THE CHRONICLES OF RANDALL | BOOK THREE

A RUNE IN TIME

LEN BOSWELL

Black Rose Writing | Texas

This is a work of fiction. Names, characters, businesses, places, events, and incidents are either the products of the author's imagination or used in a fictitious manner. Any resemblance to actual persons, living or dead, or actual events is purely coincidental.

ISBN: 978-1-68513-533-1
LIBRARY OF CONGRESS CONTROL NUMBER: 2024942337
PUBLISHED BY BLACK ROSE WRITING
www.blackrosewriting.com

Printed in the United States of America
Suggested Retail Price (SRP) $21.95

A Rune in Time is printed in Calluna

*As a planet-friendly publisher, Black Rose Writing does its best to eliminate unnecessary waste to reduce paper usage and energy costs, while never compromising the reading experience. As a result, the final word count vs. page count may not meet common expectations.

To all I love without condition
To all I love without omission

Never doubt

And especially to my Rat Terrier, Cinder, AKA "The Blur." R.I.P.

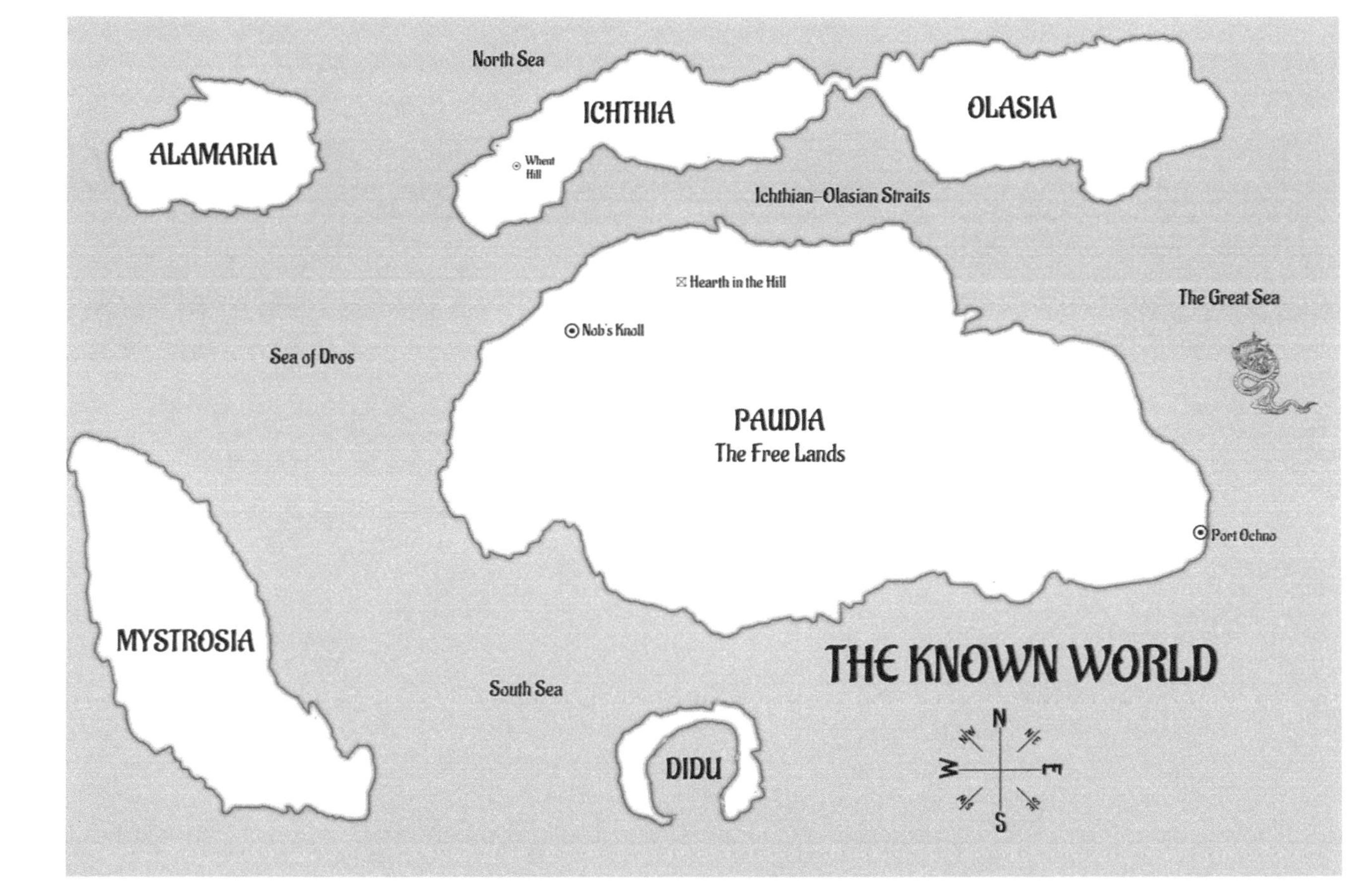
THE KNOWN WORLD
ALAMARIA
ICHTHIA
OLASIA
MYSTROSIA
DIDU
PAUDIA
The Free Lands
North Sea
Sea of Dros
South Sea
The Great Sea
Ichthian—Olasian Straits
Wheat Hill
Nob's Knoll
Hearth in the Hill
Port Ochno

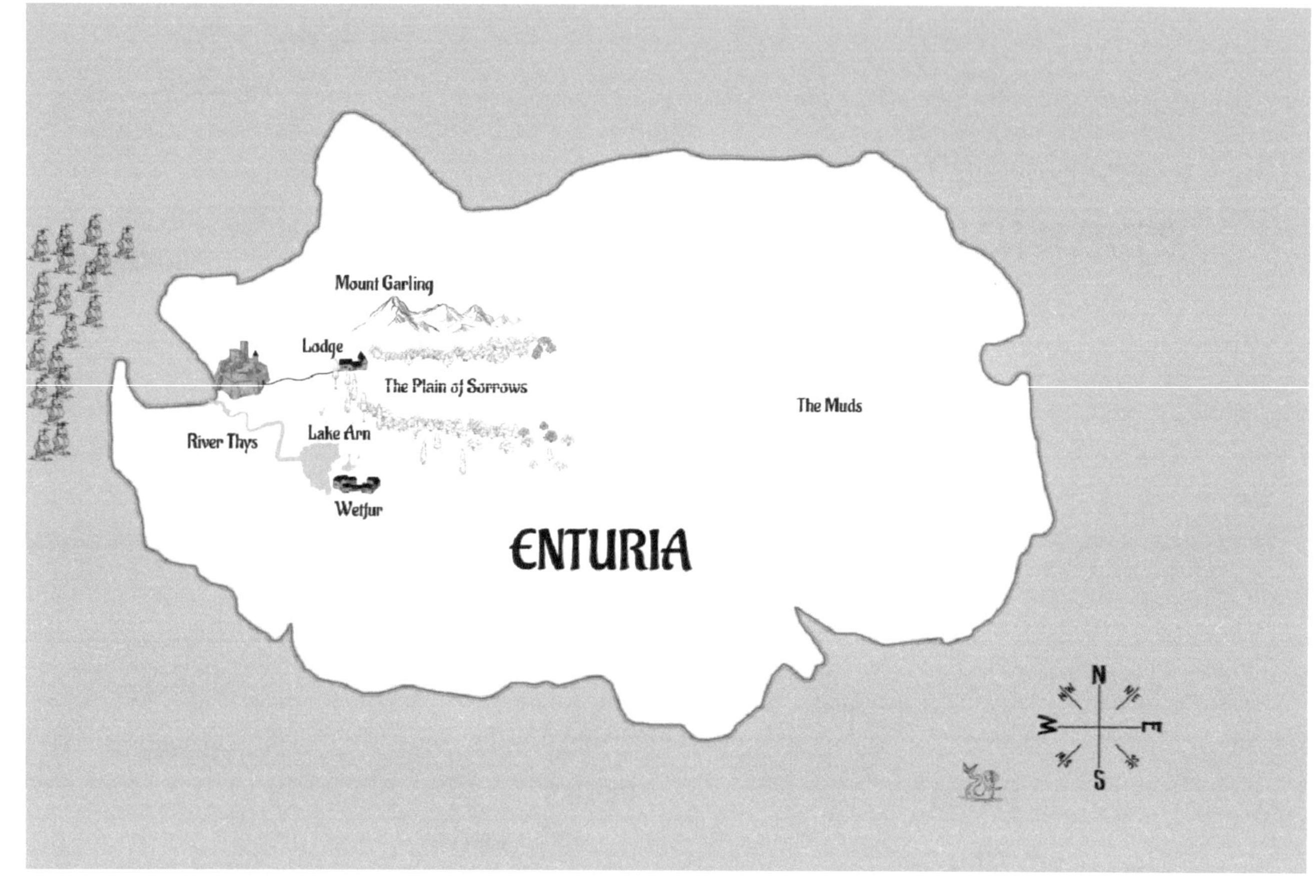

Mount Garling
Lodge
The Plain of Sorrows
River Thys
Lake Arn
Wetfur
ENTURIA
The Muds
N
W
E
S

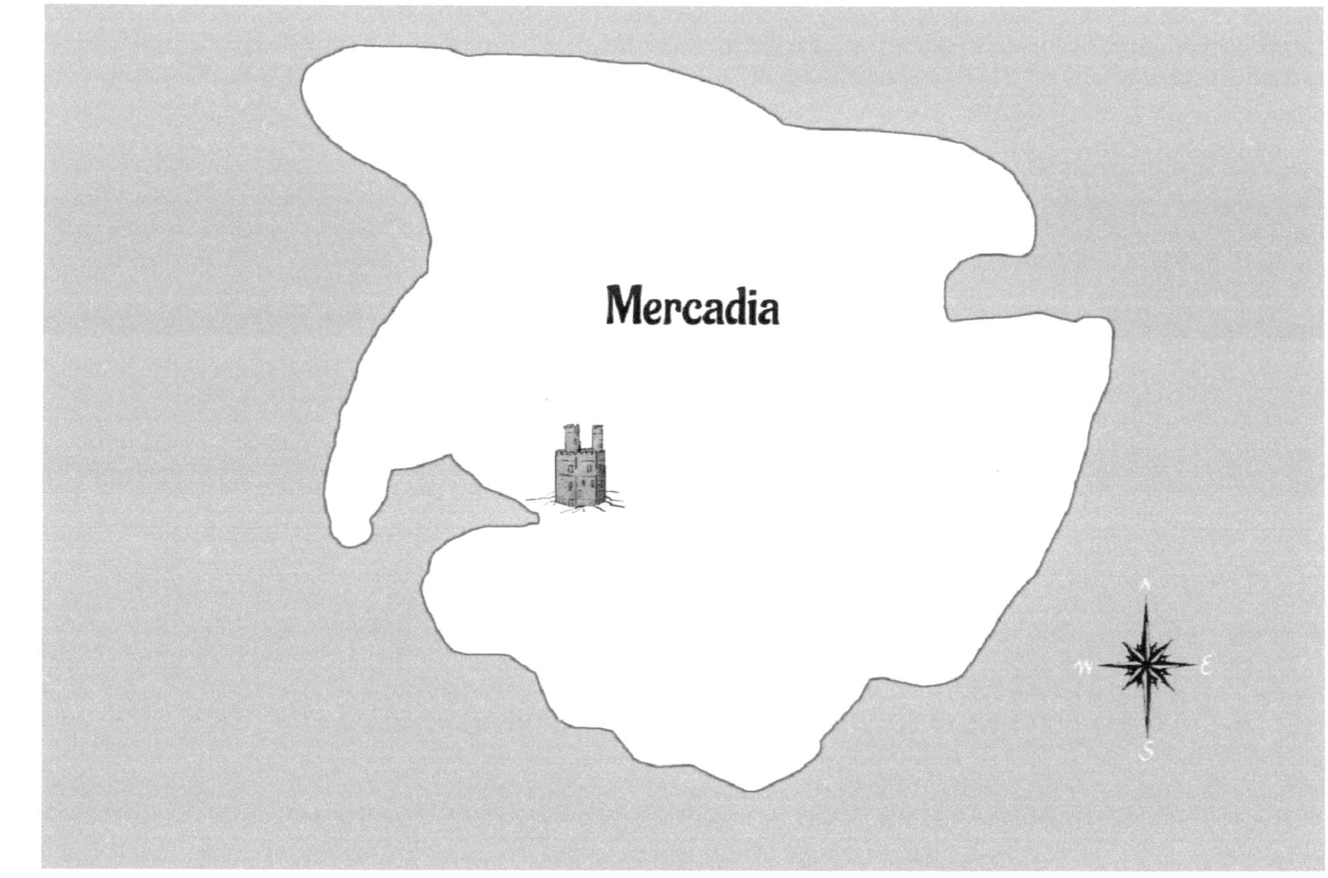

Mercadia
N
W
E
S

A RUNE IN TIME

List of Characters

Enturia

Queen Rhynt
Baron Bookins, formerly the king's fool
Lord Braque, formerly King Braque
Calax Halfhand, a sellsword, Supreme Commander of the Armies
Gash, Calax Halfhand's warhorse
Blusk, a sellsword, Master of Foot
Phendour, a sellsword, Master of Archers
Zyrx, a blacksmith and armorer
The Red Monk, d'Abo Pourcrey
Bebo, a Paudian troll
Orthor "Dreedle" Billibuck, Language Meister to the Queen
Priss, a handmaiden and archer
Cresh, Bookins' manservant
General Boh, former High Commander of the Forces of the King
Besbo d'Arc, Chancellor of Coin
Daneyh, Elf Queen
Marthe, captain of the good ship *Marthe*
The Hill Tigers: Mela Mila, and Spook

Mystrosia

King Merek the Mighty
The White Monk, d'Porto Saleen
Ci, a concubine

Ichthia

King Pandine the Third, King of Kings

Olasia

King Wazapor IV, Esteemed Ruler of Olasia

Mercadia

King Balus III

The Gods

Whelan the Wanderer, Randall Himself, God of Gods
Abo, the Red God
Porto, the White God
Canto, the Blue God
Bedo, the Green God
Dado, the Gray God
Indo, the Black God

The Elves

Queen Daneyh
Clessus, High Commander of the Armies
Slathen, Captain of the First Guard

"In a dilemma, it is helpful to change any variable, then reexamine the problem."
–Robert A. Heinlein

"The dilemma is that if one does not risk anything one risks even more."
–Erica Jong

"You don't know what you don't know."
–Socrates

"Know what you do not know."
–Gautama Buddha

Prologue

The voices seemed to be coming from every direction and in great number, and he knew one of the voices was his and all of the voices were his, just as he knew that wherever he looked, where all of him looked, all that he saw was different perspectives on the same thing: a white crow wheeling above him, squawking. And then the squawk became a single word: *come!*

Indo, the Black God, recognized the voice. "Porto?"

"None other," said the White God.

"What's happening? I seem to be everywhere."

Porto tried his best not to laugh at the sight of what must have been a thousand little Indos, all speaking as one. "Indeed, you are, the result of an unfortunate run-in with ravenous local beasts."

"They ate me?" said the horde of Indos.

"Yes, they did."

"So I am, um . . ."

Porto nodded. "Yes, the aftermath of digestion."

All the Indos sniffed at themselves. "By the gods!"

Porto laughed. "Speaking of gods, we have to be on our way."

"To join the battle?"

Porto laughed even harder. "No, what battle there was did not end in our favor. In fact, I myself was killed, if only briefly."

"Killed? How?"

"The usual, an arrow to the hand."

"I hate that imperfection."

"As do I. I find these brief periods in darkness a bit unsettling."

"As did I." He looked around. "As did *we*."

Porto chuckled. "Indeed. Anyway, come. We are to meet up with Randall and the others at the cave."

Indo scratched a thousand heads. "We were defeated? How is that possible?"

"I'll explain along the way. For now, try to pull yourself together."

Indo rolled a thousand sets of eyes and then began to do just that. "By the gods!"

Part I

Losing. *I dislike the word immensely and intensely. It is not becoming of a god, particularly a god such as myself, the supreme god Randall. But we lost. Neither fair nor square, but we lost, to that damned fool Bookins, who has not heard the last from me. Oh, no. Still, he's the least of my problems now. The so-called language meister to the queen, just a mere boy, is close to unraveling the runes in The Cave of the Six Arrows and Randall's Cave. Or at least he thinks he may have figured it all out. At any rate, he's close to a solution, and I won't permit that. Not now, not ever.*

Orthor "Dreedle" Billibuck, age twelve, was kicking himself for sending the pigeon. He was so certain he'd solved the puzzle that he had written a brief message boasting of his discovery, tied the message to the pigeon's leg, and sent it on its way.

Now he'd have to live with the embarrassment, and would no doubt lose the queen's trust. They'd all be calling him *Dreedle* again. All over a cockeyed rune.

Viewed straight on, it meant one thing, the thing he had boasted of in the message, that the cave runes showed the future, not the past. Viewed slightly askew—as it clearly was; he could see that now—it meant something completely different. But what? He could be close to a solution, or years and years away. He would have to go back to Randall's Cave and start over again, giving great care to the orientation of each rune. Was it perfectly vertical or did it tilt, and by how much? And how did the orientation of one rune compare to the orientations of the runes around it? There would be so much to consider.

He took in a deep breath and sighed. The remaining pigeon cocked its head and cooed in response, attracting Orthor's attention.

"Of course, of course," he said. "I'll send another message."

He jumped to his feet and raced over to the large boulder he used as a desk. "Yes, a second message will be just the thing."

He grabbed a small scrap of parchment, dipped his quill into the pool of ink, and began writing. It only took seconds, and seconds later he blotted it dry before turning back to the pigeon. "Come, time to go, little one. Your friend has a head start, but I think you can catch him. Bookins said you were fast."

He picked up the bird and tied the message onto its leg with a piece of loose string he'd pulled from his breeches. "Let's go!"

He raced to the mouth of the cave and tossed the bird into the air. "God speed!"

He watched as the pigeon climbed higher and higher and disappeared over the rim of the canyon.

Orthor sighed with relief. All could still be well. He turned and looked back into the cave. "A lot to do, a lot to do."

But first he'd have a fire and a well-roasted cave rat, a diet that had already added pounds to his once thin frame. His pallor, once ghostly, was now rosy, and his once flat belly was now round and growing rounder.

He walked back into the cave and began pulling together the kindling and logs for the fire, glancing back only briefly at the cave opening. "Fly fast, my little friend. Fly fast."

A flash of lightning startled him.

A shudder of pleasure ran through Baron Bookins as he eased himself into the steaming bath water. "By the gods, Cresh, this is perfect."

Cresh, his manservant, continued pouring the hot water. "Just ring the bell here if it cools too quickly," he said. "I have another bucket on the fire."

The contrast between the two could not have been more pronounced: Bookins old and frail and mostly bald, Cresh robust and twenty years younger, with flaxen hair pulled back into a ponytail; Bookins thin and short, Cresh also thin, but two heads taller. Bookins normally proportioned, Cresh big-headed and hunched.

Bookins sighed. "The way I feel now, I might be ringing the bell all day. This is wonderful."

Cresh finished pouring. "There. Will there be anything else, m'lord?"

Bookins looked around. The bell was on a small table within reach, as was a full glass of Alamarian wine and a pitcher he knew contained more. "No, bless you, I have all I need."

Cresh bowed. "If not . . ."

"Yes, the bell." He waved his hand. "Well, then, off with you."

Cresh bowed again, turned, and left the room, closing the door behind him.

Bookins sighed and sank deeper into the tub, his head resting on the back of the rim, the water lapping at his chin. Every pain receded. Every care disappeared.

He pulled the washcloth out of the water and placed it over his face. There was only him now, and the heat.

Oh, he thought, *and the wine.*

He pulled off the washcloth, picked up the glass, and took a sip, and then another. Now the warmth was growing inside him. He took a third sip, replaced the glass, and sank back down in the water. *This is too perfect, too perfect.*

But why shouldn't it be? The Mystrosians had been defeated. His gambit, though not perfect, had worked well enough for victory. And the victory had brought him praise from Queen Rhynt, along with a fine medal and an increased stipend that would carry him through the rest of his life.

He picked up the glass and took two more sips. The bath seemed to be cooling a bit, but he only needed a few more minutes anyway. He drained the glass, then chuckled.

"Those poor Mystrosians," he said, then grunted. "Well, they deserved it." The terms were unconditional. The remaining Mystrosian soldiers, along with King Merek and his retinue, were on their way back to Mystrosia, their fleet now in the hands of Enturian seamen, led by Phendour and Blusk. They had orders to see the Mystrosians safely back to their homeland and then return with all the Mystrosian ships. Enturia now had a fleet second to none.

He thought of the queen and her intentions. The fleet would not be used for waging war, but for exploration. There had always been rumors of other lands, and Queen Rhynt had a mind to find them. She had, in fact, dispatched a dozen of the newly acquired ships on a mission to the east, led by Calax Halfhand and Marthe, with the good ship *Marthe* as their flagship.

She had asked the troll Bebo to accompany Calax, but Bebo had other ideas. He wanted to return to Paudia to make sure the Mystrosians would never be able to overrun Paudia again. In the end, the queen granted him his wish. The trolls had wasted no time diving into the water and swimming for their homeland.

As for herself, the queen had taken her leave and returned to the castle, leaving Bookins and Lord Braque to their well-deserved retirement.

A sound from outside the door startled him. "Cresh, is that you?"

The door swung open and Cresh walked in, an empty bucket swinging from his hand. "Sorry, m'lord. Dropped the bucket. A bit of a flood out there."

Bookins laughed. "Never mind. My body is suitably puffed and pale and pocked. Another few minutes, and I'd have dissolved entirely."

"Yes, m'lord."

"Bring my robe. I need to get dressed for dinner. Lord Braque and I have much to discuss."

"Yes, of course, but when you're dressed, you should probably see to your pigeons."

"Pigeons? What's wrong with my pigeons?"

"Nothing, m'lord, it's just that you now have one more of them, and it seems to be carrying messages."

Bookins' eyes grew wide. "Must be Dreedle." He turned to Cresh. "My clothes, man. Get me my clothes."

Cresh set the bucket down and scurried across the room. "Over here, m'lord, over here."

"Cresh, by the gods, my robe first!"

3

Whelan the Wanderer, Randall Himself, God of Gods had had enough. "Silence!"

The assembled gods stopped their bickering immediately, some looking down, some looking up, and some looking vaguely away in various directions.

"Better," said Whelan. "Now, do each of you understand your new instructions?" He nodded at Abo, the Red God, who was still insisting on taking the form of a beautiful woman.

"Yes," she said. "I am to create a new war between Ichthia and Olasia."

"And why is that needed?"

"As a distraction to what the others will do."

"Good." He turned to Bedo, the Green God. "And you?"

"I take down Calax and his so-called voyage of exploration."

"And you, Porto?" said Whelan.

The White God sneered. "The fleet returning the Mystrosian warriors. And thank you for that. I will be able to extract some revenge on that archer who took me down."

"Good," said Whelan. "Happy hunting." He turned to Canto, the Blue God. "Canto?"

"To encourage Alamaria to strike out at the weakened Mystrosians."

"Good," said Whelan. "And how about you, Dado?"

The Gray God smiled, then chuckled. "The trolls specifically, and Paudia in general, with the help of Indo."

"Excellent," said Whelan, then turned to Indo. "Glad to see you back in one piece."

Indo smiled. "It was a strange experience, and I'm glad it's over."

"Well, be vigilant so it doesn't happen again."

Indo nodded. "And what of you, Whelan? What will be your part in this plan?"

Whelan sighed and looked at each of them. "I will take down Enturia and have my revenge on that fool." He sighed again. "But first I must deal with that young man trying to solve the riddle of these runes. He could ruin everything."

The Red God cleared her throat. "Why not just kill him?"

"If it comes to it, but not yet. I enjoy the way his mind works."

The Red God rolled her eyes. "Have your fun then, but don't wait too long."

Whelan glared at her. "I'll decide that, not you."

The Red God nodded quickly. "Of course, of course."

Whelan clapped his hands. "Go then, all of you. Make me proud."

Each disappeared in turn, leaving Whelan alone in Randall's Cave. He walked over to the boulder Orthor was using as a makeshift desk and picked up one of the scrolls. "Scribbles, and of no account."

He dropped the scroll and began walking to the cave entrance. "I think I'll find him in The Cave of the Six Arrows. Let's see what he's found."

And with that he disappeared.

4

The fire in the hearth crackled and snapped, drawing Queen Rhynt's attention away from her guest, the elf queen Daneyh, who sat opposite her, going on and on with praise for Rhynt and Bookins. Rhynt didn't know what to make of her. She had kept herself hidden during the battle, and her very existence had been a surprise to everyone.

"To be so successful at such a young age, well, it is unheard of in my world within the tower. Why, I was in my fifties before I had to face war. And now, look at you, a mere babe, queen for but a few days—and you win, you win!"

Rhynt smiled back at the woman, who could have been a vision of Rhynt's future self, save for the elf queen's pointed ears. They shared red hair, though Daneyh's was streaked with white, and their eyes were deep green, though Daneyh's had become rheumy over the years. One thing they did not share, of course, was a metal calf and foot like Rhynt's. And Rhynt's green merilium armor was in sharp contrast to the other queen's white, gold-trimmed gown and matching slippers.

Rhynt sighed. "It was Bookins' doing, not mine."

Daneyh clucked. "But you *approved* the plan. Had you not, well . . . ."

Had she? Rhynt wondered. The sudden appearance of the trolls was as much a surprise to her as it was to the poor Mystrosians. "Just in general, not the details."

"Still, a good *decision*, one that won the day." She leaned forward and whispered. "My dear, in the end, it's not what you do, but what you decide. You're a leader, a natural, a—"

Rhynt had to interrupt. "Queen Daneyh, I thank you for your words, and it has been wonderful meeting with you and having this talk, but—"

Daneyh could interrupt as well as Rhynt, perhaps better. "But," she said, raising a finger above her head. "But you have more important things to do." She began to stand.

"Wait, sit."

Daneyh sat back down.

"You talk of decisions," said Rhynt, "and I would have your wisdom about the ones I have made in the last few hours."

"Decisions?"

"Yes," said Rhynt. She sighed, then described what she had done: sent Calax on a voyage of exploration, sent Phendour and Blusk to Mystrosia, to return their warriors, and allowed the trolls to return home to Paudia.

Daneyh listened carefully to it all, occasionally taking a sip of wine and glancing over at Rhynt's hill tigers, who snored softly near the warmth of the hearth.

"So," said Rhynt. "What do you think?"

Daneyh took a last sip of wine and set her glass down on the table. "I agree with everything except your voyages of exploration."

"Oh?"

"Yes, not that it isn't noble—and something that should be done. But my dear, you've sent your best warrior to sea at a fragile time."

"What do you mean?"

"You've defeated Mystrosia, yes. You've taken its ships, yes. You have, in effect, taken them off the board when it comes to power. Yes, yes, and yes." She raised her finger again. "But . . ."

"Yes?"

"You've forgotten about the consequences of your victory. What will other countries do? Alamaria has been under the Mystrosian thumb for years. What will they do? Will they be an ally or an enemy?"

"Oh, I hadn't thought about that."

"And what about Ichthia and Olasia?"

"I see, I see," said Rhynt.

"Do you? Do you realize that this victory has exposed Enturia? No one knew you even existed before the Mystrosians found you. The Alamarians, the Ichthians, the Olasians—they'll all come. The question is when and for what purpose? To establish relations or to conquer you?"

Rhynt sighed. "I did not realize."

"But there's more, dear, there's more."

"What?"

"Paudia, the Free Lands, would make a sweet prize. It's ripe for conquest and, save for the trolls, it's defenseless."

Rhynt leaned forward. "What shall I do?"

Queen Daneyh smiled and raised her finger again. "Here's what I'd do. First, rest easy about Paudia. It has always been our intent to return to Paudia. That is our home. We will set up outposts at the ports and other key defensive positions so that Paudia is never overrun again."

"But it will remain the free lands, correct?"

Queen Daneyh rolled her eyes. "Of course, dear. We elves view ourselves as guardians of the free lands, not masters. All will be welcome, all will be free—but we will not permit invasions."

Rhynt nodded. "Very well, what else?"

"You and your monk should send gelas to Mystrosia, Alamaria, Ichthia, and Olasia."

"I had thought to send ambassadors."

Queen Daneyh gave her head a quick shake. "No, it's too soon for that. They will question your intentions. And yes, I know your intentions are peaceful, but they will be suspicious. No, send gelas to get a sense of the impact of your victory on those at court, as well as the lowest citizens. And then deal with what you discover."

"Okay, that makes sense. I will meet with the Red Monk as soon as we are finished here."

"Good, now, as for the Mystrosian fleet, go forward as planned, with one small change. Tell your captains, Phendour and Blusk, to return to Enturia by the northern route, not the southern."

"That is a long way. Why would we do that?"

"A show of force. If they take the northern route, they will pass by the southern coasts of Alamaria, Ichthia, and Olasia."

"But force is not my intention."

"Of course, and you will not do anything provocative. But let them see the size and power of your fleet. If they ever had intentions to attack Enturia, that fleet will give them pause."

"I see."

"And if your gelas sense that ambassadors would be a good idea, then Phendour and Blusk can handle that task."

Rhynt nodded. "Yes, that would be good. Anything else?"

"Yes, you should send a gela to Calax Halfhand and have him head north, toward Olasia."

"Olasia?"

"Yes, if an ambassador is needed in either Ichthia or Olasia, there will be none better than the hero of the Battle of Whent Hill. They fear him *and* respect him."

"But the exploration."

"If all goes well, he can return to it immediately. If not . . ."

"He will return to Enturia."

"Exactly, to defend it once more."

Rhynt smiled at her. "Queen Daneyh, I thank you for your advice. It is both wise and thorough."

Queen Daneyh nodded, then stood, extending her hand. "Thank you, I hope it serves. Now, I must take my leave. The tower leaves in but an hour."

"So soon?"

"We are eager to get to Paudia."

"I understand you will be taking Zyrx with you."

"Yes, but only to see him home to the Hearth in the Hill. He has done so much for us, after all."

"I will miss him."

"He said he will be stopping by to make his farewells."

"I shall look forward to it."

Queen Daneyh started for the door, then turned. "Oh, one thing more. Your new crown, the one that speaks to you."

"Yes?"

"Listen to it, *always.*"

"It has helped me so far."

Queen Daneyh smiled. "As it should. However, a time will come when the advice given by the voice seems wrong. Do not think so. It is always right."

"I'm sure everything will be fine."

Queen Daneyh raised her eyebrows. "Oh, so far, yes, but a time will come, and you can count on it, when the voice will ask you to do something against your best judgment. It may even ask you to strike someone down."

Now it was Rhynt's turn to raise her eyebrows. "Truly?"

"The voice has no politics. It's only goal is to protect the wearer—at *any* cost, my dear."

"I shall keep that in mind."

Queen Daneyh smiled, nodded, and then walked away.

Rhynt watched her go. *I must talk to Zyrx about this*, she thought.

"Listen to the queen," said the voice in the crown. "Zyrx knows nothing."

5

She lifted into the air effortlessly, her wings growing stronger with each flap, shaking off the long wait in the cave. Flight, this is what she was made for, the feel of the air rushing over her wings and body, exhilarating her, lifting her higher and higher. The first flash of lightning was a surprise, forcing her down, but the second was just another bolt, easily ignored, her wings helping her gain altitude. She knew the rain was coming, but rain was never a problem for her.

And come it did, torrents of rain pounding her, but she met it with strength, easily maintaining a safe altitude. She looked below her, the ground racing below her. A plain in all directions, hardly a bush or tree. And then hours later a small town, hard up against the sea. She had heard Orthor mention its name more than once. Port Ochno, Paudia's eastern port on The Great Sea. A few people were scurrying around, racing through the rain for shelter.

She looked out to sea. There would be nothing but water below her now, and hours more of this storm, which raged and raged, the sea rolling in swells deep enough to swallow even the largest vessel.

She looked back. The land was receding, disappearing into darkness and the shroud of the storm. Now all her thoughts were to keep going, to stay calm, to push closer to Enturia with each flap of her wings. She thought of her mate, somewhere ahead in the comfort of a coop she had never seen.

The lightning flashed again and again.

6

Bookins stood in front of the mirror for far too long, turning this way and that, in awe of his new baronial clothing. The stockings, the cape, the waistcoat, all were a plush purple, in fabrics soft to the touch and warm. Cresh caught him looking.

"They are fine, m'lord, and if I may say so, they fit you perfectly."

Startled at being discovered preening in front of a mirror, Bookins quickly backed away and turned for the door. "I have to see about my pigeons."

"Yes, m'lord, of course, m'lord."

Bookins scurried from the room, leaving the chuckles of Cresh behind him. "Dastardly man. A snoop. I'll have to watch him carefully. Sneaking up on me like that."

The pain in his knees forced him to slow his pace. "And the pigeons are so far away. I should move the coop."

He pressed on. Fortunately, the lodge that had come with his ascent to a barony was smaller than the castle, and the oak floors were much softer than the slabs of stone he'd had to tread all those years as a fool.

A few more strides and he was outside, the coop in sight. He had had it built in the days before the battle against the Mystrosians. It was a simple affair, a rectangular building built from swamp pine and black alder, with enough room for over a hundred pigeons, though there were only twenty or so now. He would increase their number as quickly as he could.

Their cooing grew louder as he approached, each trying to get his attention in a language Bookins didn't understand.

It took him a while to spot the pigeon with the message attached to its leg, but it took no time to scoop him up and remove the wet parchment wrapped around its leg.

"What do we have here?" *Must be from Dreedle,* he thought, *that strange boy the queen had entrusted with a mission to decipher the runes in some caves in Paudia.*

He unrolled the parchment and tried his best to make out what was written on it. "Unbelievable," he said. "It seems he knows nothing of inks."

He squinted at the parchment. "*Ig?* And '*age*' at the end, I think. The rest is just a blur."

He held it up to the light, but could not parse out any other letters. "*Ig* something something *age.*"

He thought about it. "There's a little smudge after *ig*, so perhaps the word is *ignore.* Yes, that must be it. I mean it could say *igmot,* but why would Dreedle send a message about a small flightless bird?" He thought of other possibilities—*ignite, ignorant, ignominious, ignoble*—and then shook his head. "No, the word is *ignore,* I'm sure of it."

He looked at the parchment once more. "And it ends in *age,* with something in the middle. Not much, a couple of small words, or perhaps one longer word."

His eyes went wide. "Of course, it says ignore something something *message.* Message, absolutely *message.*"

He sighed. "But what message? This message? Another message?"

He turned back to the pigeons in the coop, searching for another bird with a message.

Nothing.

He looked up, hoping to see a pigeon about to land, but the sky was birdless.

"Curious," he said. "Very, very curious."

"What's curious," said a voice behind him.

Bookins turned and smiled at Lord Braque. "I have received a curious message, all but washed away by last night's storm."

Lord Braque held out his hand. "Let me see."

Bookins handed the wet parchment to him. "I think it says *ignore something message*."

Lord Braque held it up to the light, then grunted. "I see that, yes, but I also see the word in the middle, or most of it. It says *ignore previous message*."

Bookins blinked. "Previous? But there has been only the one bird."

Lord Braque looked up at the sky. "Perhaps the second bird overtook the first, or as I warned you on our trip here, perhaps the first bird landed farther west, at the castle. You had barely trained them, after all."

Bookins sighed and shook his head. "I must send two birds, then. One to the castle and one to Dreedle."

"Sounds right. Do you think he discovered something, about those runes, I mean."

Bookins shrugged. "Maybe, but whatever he found, he had second thoughts about it. He thought one thing, perhaps exciting news, but then realized he'd made a mistake and sent this second bird." He looked over at the bird. "Yes, it's one of my fastest. It would have had no problem catching up with the other bird I sent along with him."

"You better hurry, then. We can't have Queen Rhynt acting on a message that's not true."

Bookins nodded. "Come then, we can break fast while I pen the messages." He grunted, then rolled his eyes. "With ink that *won't* wash away."

7

Orthor sat in front of the fire, shivering. The winds of the storm had reached even here, buffeting the fire this way and that, whatever warmth it offered blown away.

And then the winds stopped. Just stopped. There in all their fierceness one second and gone the next.

"There, that's better," said a voice behind him.

Orthor didn't have to turn to know whose it was—the Red God's, deep and sultry, a voice that seemed to command and entice all at once. Now a different kind of shiver raced up his spine. He turned and stood to face her. "You."

"Indeed, me."

She had had red hair and green eyes the last time she appeared before him, but this time her hair was raven black and her eyes the palest violet. Her clothing was the same, a sleek, body-hugging red dress and a matching cloak that reached to the floor of the cave.

"Why are you here?" he said. He knew his voice was quavering, but the combination of the cold and the god's sudden appearance prevented him from speaking without his lips trembling.

"Here now," she said. "Let's get you warmed up." She took off her cloak and wrapped it around his shoulders. Then she pointed at the fire and mumbled words that made the flames grow higher. "There, that's better. Now, sit down by the fire and let us have a little chat about our agreement."

Orthor blinked. He remembered it well, and what it required him to do to keep Queen Rhynt from harm. When he had solved the runes, he was to notify the Red God first. He had only to say the three words she had whispered in his ear, and she would appear. He had not said the words, but here she was. "Our agreement?"

The Red God's laugh was almost a cackle. "Oh, dear boy, don't play dumb with me. You know full well the terms of our agreement, which I must point out, you have violated."

Orthor tried to walk back to the fire, but he kept tripping on the long cloak.

The Red God laughed again, but the cackle was now a derisive guffaw. "Stand still."

Orthor stopped struggling with the cloak.

She touched the cloak on one shoulder and it began to shrink.

"What's happening," said Orthor.

She snapped at him. "Stay still!"

Orthor obeyed and so did the cloak, shrinking quickly to a size that fit Orthor perfectly. "This is wonderful," he said, "and it's so warm."

"Well, of course it is." She grabbed him by the shoulders and forced him down. "Now sit, here."

Orthor dropped down hard on the ground. "Hey!"

"Don't hey me, you little traitor."

"But I—"

"No, don't try to wiggle your way out of this. You sent a pigeon to the queen."

Orthor started to object, but the Red God pulled a pigeon out of thin air and dropped it in front of Orthor.

"This pigeon." She snapped her fingers, and a small piece of parchment appeared in her hand. "With this message."

Orthor looked from the pigeon to the parchment. "No, no, you don't understand. Our agreement was to take effect when I actually found something, a workable solution. You must remember that."

The Red God chuckled sardonically. "Oh, I remember. The thing is you apparently forgot."

"No, you see—"

She thrust the message in front of his face. "What did it say?"

Orthor was confused. Had she not read the message?"

"Um . . ."

She shook the parchment in front of him. "The message is unreadable—the rain, the storm—so what did it say?"

Orthor thought fast. *She doesn't know.* "Oh, that pigeon. I sent it to Bookins, hoping he could send me more supplies. Quills, ink, more parchment, and food and clothing. Including a cloak such as this. It is wonderful and I thank you for it."

The Red God looked confused. "So you have not solved the runes?"

Orthor shook his head. "Not even close. And if I had, you would be the first person, erm, *god* to know."

"Have you solved even a little part of it?"

"I thought I had a few days ago, and thought to summon you, but I quickly realized my solution was wrong."

"Wrong?"

"The runes, you see, must be viewed in relation to the others. When the rune is straight it means one thing, when it's a little tilted to the left, it means another, and those meanings change when you consider the positioning of the adjacent runes, top, sides, bottoms, tilt, and—"

"Enough of your gibberish," she said. "I want a solution."

"And you'll have it. It will just take time."

The Red God sighed. "Something I don't have at the moment. I should be in Ichthia this very moment."

"I will work as quickly as I can."

She nodded. "Make sure you do. And remember two things: our agreement and the fact that wherever I am, I'm watching you."

He started to say don't worry, but she snapped her fingers and was gone.

He sat by the fire a few minutes longer, then moved away to pick up the bird and the parchment and bring them back to the fire. He laid down the bird gently. Its neck was broken, no doubt by the Red God. He had once seen a pigeon master kill several of his pigeons because he could no longer afford to feed them. He had simply grabbed each bird by the head and whirled their bodies around, the force snapping their necks instantly.

He looked at the bird again and shook his head. "Which one are you?" He had no idea.

"I should have paid more attention to the differences between the two of you."

He picked up the parchment and sighed. "Nothing. Just a blur.

He looked down at the bird. "I don't suppose you can tell me which message you carried? No, I didn't think so."

He wondered whether the other pigeon had made it through the storm and which message it carried. If the queen had received the first message, and could read it—there was certainly no guarantee of either—she would assume not only that Orthor had solved the riddle of the runes, but that the drawing of the girl and her tigers was a depiction of a future event, one where she was racing toward the precipice of a deep chasm. And if the queen had received the second message—ignore previous message—she would no doubt be confused.

Orthor's best hope was that either the other bird did not make it through the storm or that it had arrived with no message at all, just an unreadable smudge on parchment.

And then there was the looming dilemma. If he solved the runes and told the Red God first, he would betray his queen and put her in harm's way. And if he told the queen first, he would put himself in danger.

He wondered whether he could lie to the Red God and tell the queen the truth. Would the Red God see through such a ruse? Would the lie come out eventually and put him in danger once more? Or would he and the queen be in grave danger no matter what he told the Red God?

He sighed. "The first thing I need to do is solve the runes." *What am I saying?* he thought. *Maybe I should just give up.* "No, I will know what they say, or die in the trying."

He looked down at the bird again. "Come, let's find a nice spot to bury you. Can't have the cave rats get you."

8

Rhynt's hill tigers, Mela, Mila, and Spook, bounded across the room to greet their former owner, Zyrx, who went to his knees to hug each of them. "Oh, my friends, my wonderful friends."

Rhynt was not far behind, giving Zyrx a big hug. "Oh, it's so good to see you, Zyrx."

Zyrx smiled up at her. She seemed to have grown an inch or two, which is not usually good news for a dwarf or his neck. He was forever looking up at people, even those who didn't deserve it. And she looked softer somehow, now that the battle was over, even though she still wore her armor, armor that he had crafted in merilium just for her. "My queen." He attempted a bow, then thought better of it. "Um, my queen."

Rhynt took a step back and looked him up and down. He seemed, tired, as well he should be. Hours and hours at the forge had taken its toll. "Thanks to you."

Zyrx looked confused. "My queen?"

"What, have you forgotten the medal I hung around your neck just hours ago?"

"Oh, that."

"You are a hero of the Battle of the Plain of Sorrows."

He smiled sheepishly and looked down. "If you say so, Majesty."

"I *do* say so. Where would we have been without your armor, your wondrous merilium. And where would *I* be now without the charmed crown you crafted for me. No, don't say a word. I'd be dead is what."

"Majesty, I merely provided the tools for your victory, and the charmed gems in the crown were the idea of an elf."

"Ha! How wrong you are. No, I will not accept that. The armor, the crown, your tireless work. No, I will never forget that or tire of singing your praise."

Zyrx's face seemed to be reddening. He attempted a bow again, and failed. "Majesty, I will accept your verdict, but I am not here for praise. I wanted to tell you of my plans."

"I just met with Queen Daneyh, so I think I know a little. You are going home, to the Hearth on the Hill."

"Yes, but there's more. While I was within the tower, I had an idea."

"Don't tell me, a new application for merilium?"

"Indeed so."

"Is it secret or can you tell me?"

"Not a secret, to you at least. I have this idea, you see."

"Well?"

Zyrx sighed. "You'll think me foolish if I say it."

Rhynt walked over and gave him a hug. "There is nothing you could say that I would take as foolish."

"Very well. What are ships made of, Majesty?"

"Wood, of course." She suddenly realized where he was going. "Wait, you would use *merilium* instead? No, that's not possible. The ship would sink from the weight."

Zyrx shook his head. "I think otherwise, Majesty, and I plan to prove it, or at least test it on a small scale, when I get back to my hearth."

"And how would you do that? You're hearth is nowhere near the ocean."

"But I have a little stream, Majesty. I will build a small ship." He held out his hands to indicate a ship the length of his arms."

"But that would only weigh a few pounds. How would that be a test at all? A real ship made of merilium would be heavy beyond imagination."

Zyrx held up a hand. "Majesty, once I had occasion to see a warrior's shield floating down a great river. It was made of the basest of metals, far heavier than merilium, and it floated, Majesty, *floated*."

"And you truly believe it's possible?"

"Not certain. The gods have a way of tricking us when we're dead certain about something, but certain enough to build a little merilium ship. And, of course, you would be the first to know of its success or failure."

Rhynt nodded.

"Imagine it, Majesty, a fleet of ships made of merilium. Enturia would be invincible."

Rhynt frowned. "I have no plans for war, ever again, Zyrx."

"Why that's my point, Majesty. No one would dare start a war, knowing of your fleet's power."

Rhynt cocked her head. "Do you think so?"

"Yes, does a molfrump attack a demidog?"

Rhynt smiled. "Go ahead, then. Test your theory, and if the test is successful, I will give you whatever help you need to create your invincible fleet."

"Thank you, your Majesty. I will take my leave, then."

"You will be sailing back to Paudia in the tower, with Queen Daneyh?"

"Yes, Majesty. A few days within the tower will be but seconds in Enturian time. I will be able to do a lot of work on the voyage."

"You will have your model in short order, then."

"No, not really. I will build nothing when I am within the tower. I will just think about what I need to do, leaving the actual work to my return to my hearth."

"What? Why not get it done while you're in the tower?"

Zyrx sighed. "Sorry, your Majesty, but I do not altogether trust the elves."

Rhynt was startled. "And why is that?"

"It's hard for me to put my finger on it, Majesty. They ask too many questions, for one thing."

"Questions?"

"About merilium, about blacksmithing . . ."

"That seems harmless enough. They needed to know blacksmithing to help you forge our weapons and armor."

"Oh, it goes beyond that, Majesty. Questions about you, as well, and Calax, Phendour, and Blusk, among others. Bookins, of course, and the former king."

Rhynt frowned. "I see. Tell me, why is it that *today* is the first time I became aware that there was such a person as Queen Daneyh?"

Zyrx rolled his eyes. "Tell me about it. I knew there was such a person, but I did not meet her until after our victory. Until then, she was nowhere to be seen."

Rhynt shook her head. "Curious. She does not strike me as a ruler who would hide in the background. She seemed, well, outspoken. Full of advice. It's hard to believe she would have had nothing to offer by way of strategy for our battle with the Mystrosians."

"Aye, Majesty."

"Tell me, before she appeared, who was giving you orders or at least representing the elves?"

Zyrx shrugged. "No one, really. They took me in and pretty much left me to my own devices. Setting up the forges, training the new elf blacksmiths, all of it they left to me. Once, I believe, I talked briefly with a captain in the guard, but he certainly wasn't in charge of me."

"What about the wizard?"

"Who?"

"Oh, that's right, you weren't with us when we first encountered the wizard. As soon as I touched the side of the tower, he popped out and began helping us cross a river in Paudia. He was swept away with Blusk and Phendour, but I assumed since they survived, he did, too. Is that not the case?"

Zyrx shrugged. "There was no such wizard within the tower when I went in, so he must have been swept away."

Rhynt sighed. "Very curious."

"Indeed."

Rhynt nodded. "Tell you what. Will you do me a favor?"

"Anything, Majesty."

"I'd like you to be my eyes and ears when you travel to Paudia. Talk to the elves you trust about the queen, about the tower, about the witch."

Zyrx's eyes went wide. "Wait, what? What witch?"

Rhynt started to reply, but the Red Monk, d'Abo Pourcrey, burst into the room. "Majesty, there's been a bird. News from Baron Bookins."

"News?" said Rhynt. "About what?"

"He says he received a message from that boy Dreedle."

Rhynt turned to Zyrx. "Oh, how wonderful. He said he would send me a message as soon as he solved the runes in Randall's Cave and the Cave of the Six Arrows." She turned back to the Red Monk. "Go on."

"The message he received said to ignore any message that came to us here."

Rhynt frowned. "Have we received a message, d'Abo?"

"No, Majesty."

"What do you think it could mean?"

"I think perhaps there was something wrong with the message, Majesty. Perhaps your Dreedle made a mistake."

"A mistake?"

"Thought he had solved the runes or some such, and then discovered he was wrong."

"So, one pigeon for the message and a second pigeon for the correction."

"Yes, that's how I see it, Majesty."

Rhynt sighed. "This will not do. I must know more."

The Red Monk turned his hands palms up. "Well, majesty, without the bird and its message, I'm afraid—"

"No, I'm not just giving up. I would know what that message said." She turned to Zyrx. "When does the tower leave for Paudia."

"In but an hour," said Zyrx.

She turned to d'Abo. "I want you in that tower."

The Red Monk seemed shocked. "Majesty!"

"Do not protest. You are to accompany Zyrx to Paudia. I want you both to stop in to see Orthor. What was in the message? Why did he seek to retrieve it? What progress has he made on the runes?"

"But Majesty," said Zyrx, "that is far afield of my planned route. I want to get started on my, um, *project* as soon as possible." He suddenly brightened. "Can't you just far-see? Or send a gela?"

The Red Monk chuckled. "The distances are too far, my friend."

Rhynt nodded. "Exactly, and pigeons are too slow, and no way to carry on a conversation."

Zyrx threw up his hands. "Very well, but we will need supplies: horses, pigeons, provisions, and the like."

Rhynt smiled, pleased. "Besbo d'Arc, Chancellor of Coin, will provide whatever you need, plus additional coin to handle whatever you might need once you land in Paudia. Orthor must be running low on supplies himself, so I'll see to it that the sum of coin you receive will help you transport provisions to him as well."

The Red Monk nodded. "And for the return trip, Majesty?"

She shook her head. "There will be no return trip, at least not immediately."

The Red Monk looked like someone had just swung an axe at him. "What? What do you mean no return trip?"

"Zyrx will accompany you to Randall's Cave, but after assuring Orthor's safety, he will proceed home, to the Hearth in the Hill. You, however, shall stay with Orthor."

"But Majesty, I had planned to do so much more here now that the war is over."

She shook her head. "No, you shall do as I say. I want you to protect Orthor. I fear for his safety." She put a hand on his shoulder. "This is important, d'Abo. I fear our so-called war is but the first battle in something bigger. I need you to protect him and to send whatever news he has about the runes."

"What, by pigeon? I thought you rejected that."

"Indeed, but not completely. Send me brief messages by pigeon but more detailed information and news by courier."

"Courier? Where am I going to find a courier?"

Rhynt knew exactly. "There is an archer named Priss. I will have her select a team of couriers, enough to handle the back and forth. All will be battle ready and swift. How many do you think we'll need?"

The Red Monk stroked his chin. *Two days at sea, two on land, each way—and of course enough horses and ships and sailors to provide passage.* "Majesty, I'd say at least six couriers, not to mention the ships and crew. It's going to be very expensive."

"Losing Enturia would be a greater expense. No, let's go with a dozen couriers and everything they'll need."

Zyrx, who had been silent throughout this exchange, spoke up. "Majesty, we have but an hour to get ourselves and the couriers and supplies into the tower."

"Yes, I realize that."

"But you forget something. The passage of time within the tower is different from our time. In Tower Time, it will take about two years to reach Paudia. I only mention this because it will give us time to get organized, train, and so on."

Rhynt smiled. "Wonderful! Now go, both of you. I will see to it that Priss and her couriers meet you at the tower within the hour."

Part Two

The future flows out of the present—and the past—and is twisted by man, gods, and events, a chaotic struggle to choose direction and fix outcomes, whether for good or for evil. And I am always at the forefront. No, that is not quite accurate. I am everywhere all at once, molding and shaping events with invisible hands, but sure hands, like a sculptor transforming mere clay into wonders to behold. Yes, Enturia won that first battle, but who's to say that wasn't part of my plan all along? Come then, as the world begins to shake once more.

9

Porto, the White God, stood at the top of the caldera of Dido, looking down and watching what few survivors had struggled out of the sea. There were not many, perhaps a dozen. All the ships in the once mighty Mystrosian fleet were either sunk or floating mastless and without direction in the warm waters of the South Sea, pepper sharks swirling around the few sailors clinging to the toppled masts or gift-wrapped in the tangled halyards.

He had waited to start the storm until the fleet was just north of Dido, a once proud land destroyed in fire and ash just twenty years ago, leaving only a crescent of land and a large harbor.

Whelan would be pleased by Porto's work, although he would probably quibble at the number of survivors. Porto would be ready with his usual defense: *if you don't have survivors, who will tell the tale? Come, Whelan, as a part-time minstrel you must see the importance of this.*

Porto smiled, then chuckled, just as he would when he next saw Whelan and boasted of his victory.

Shouts from below caught his attention. One of the survivors had spotted a mastless ship that had crashed into the rocks along the shore. There would be supplies in it, stores that they could use to prolong their survival. Perhaps they could even put the ship right again and sail away back to Enturia or onward to Mystrosia. Porto smiled at that. In fact, he could help them, if needed.

He would just have to sit and watch, and he was good at that.

10

Calax and Marthe had sailed east, then north, in the nameless sea, hoping to discover new lands or wonders to behold, perhaps the mythical land of Mercadia. But so far, there had been nothing much. A small island occupied by hundreds of what looked like large, antlered molfrumps. A curiosity, no doubt, but when they killed a few, they found that their meat was foul and their antlers brittle.

They had sailed on, the sea flat as a puddle, the wind either weak or nonexistent, the crews of the small fleet of ships now short-tempered.

And then came a glorious sunrise, the sky a brilliant scarlet with patches and streaks of orange and yellow and gray. And low on the horizon, a dark, black mass of roiling clouds.

Marthe joined Calax at the rail of the good ship *Marthe*. "There is a saying about such skies."

Calax shrugged his shoulders. "That the skies are beautiful, no doubt."

Marthe rolled his eyes. "If only. No, the saying is, red sky at night, sailor's delight; red skies at morning, sailor take warning." Marthe pointed at the dark clouds. "See that? That's a massive storm, and it's headed right for us."

"But it's so far away, Marthe. Can't we outrun her?"

Marthe shook his head and sighed. "Put a finger in your mouth and hold it up to the wind."

Calax complied. "Okay, now what?"

"Did you feel any wind?"

"Um, no."

"Because there is none."

"So . . ."

"We're going to get slammed, hard."

"So what do we do?"

"Batten down anything that could come loose and ride out the storm. I mean, unless we can make it to land, and I see none of that, either."

Calax turned in a circle, looking in all directions for even a spit of land. "Nothing."

Marthe suddenly pointed east. "There, *there!*

II

Phendour looked at Blusk. Blusk looked at Phendour. Both shook their heads and returned to surveying the scene.

They counted twelve survivors, including themselves, and the badly damaged remains of one ship, *Myst Ryder*, the flagship of the fleet. There was no sign of other ships or their crews.

All the survivors were from the Myst Ryder, save one, a concubine from the harem of King Merek the Mighty. The king himself was missing, as was the White Monk, d'Porto Saleen.

Blusk grunted as he pulled off his merilium breast shield. "Best get out of your armor, Phendour, or you'll stay wet forever."

"Aye," said Phendour as she tugged at the straps and let the armor fall to the ground. "May come in handy for serving soup."

Blusk laughed. "Well, at least you haven't lost your sense of humor."

"Lost everything else, it seems."

"Now, now, let's not get down on ourselves. We've a ship with stores and supplies, so there's no danger of dying of hunger and thirst." He dropped his voice. "For a month or so, anyway."

"I'm worried," said Phendour, scanning the horizon and seeing nothing.

Blusk scoffed. "We'll be fine, I tell you."

"It's not surviving that worries me, Blusk. It's the other ships. Did they sink or are they out there somewhere, either scattered to the winds, or worse, sailing toward Mystrosia, under the control of the Mystrosians."

Blusk nodded. "I'll take scattered, or even sunk and drowned, but the other option would be worth worrying about. Thousands of soldiers, all ready for battle, sailing in a fleet bigger than any in the known world."

"Aye," said Phendour. She turned and looked at the survivors huddled together on a rock. "So, who have we got?"

"Well, there's the concubine for distraction, four of our comrade elves, and five Mystrosian prisoners, including if I am not mistaken, our cook."

Phendour brightened. "Our cook? Wonderful! We'll need to talk to him first. He'll have a better idea of our food and water supply and how long we have."

"Ha, I'm more interested in anything we have right about now. I'm absolutely famished."

"Aye, I could go for a fresh-killed rabbit or six on a spit right about now."

"Near-death experiences will do that to you," said Blusk.

"Yes, let's have the cook turn out a meal as soon as possible. I think we'll all feel better about that."

"And then we'll have to deal with our situation."

"Yeah." She looked west along the caldera. "I lived here once. My mother died here when the volcano erupted." She pointed at a rock formation a few hundred yards away. "If memory serves, the village was just beyond those rocks. It seems unlikely, but perhaps some of the buildings survived. At least it might be worth a look. Shelter would be a good thing."

"Aye," said Blusk. "While the cook's doing his work, let's send a small party over there to see what's what."

"Sounds like a plan," said Phendour. "Let's go, or the day will be gone before we know it."

12

Queen Rhynt stood on the dock with Mela, Mila, and Spook, watching the elven tower disappear into a fog that had enveloped the docks and the castle itself, a fine mist working its way down the halls and into the rooms.

The Red Monk, Zyrx, Priss, the couriers, and all their supplies were within, along with the mysterious Queen Daneyh and her thousands of elves. Rhynt never dreamed that her first orders would lead to these consequences, that she would be essentially alone. Yes, she had soldiers around her, and a few members of the council, but everyone near and dear to her was now at sea, on missions ordered by her. She had unwittingly engineered her own isolation.

"Why so glum," said a voice behind her.

She knew instantly who it was, and spun around to greet him. "Whelan!" She gave him a big hug. "Where on earth have you been? You missed the battle. We won! It was glorious!"

Whelan laughed. "What? Did you not see me? I was everywhere, even behind the Mystrosian lines."

Rhynt's eyes widened. "Truly? No, everyone wondered what had become of you."

Whelan pulled his lute from his shoulder and gave it a strum. "Majesty, I was gathering material for songs and ballads, on heroic themes to capture your glorious victory." He strummed the lute again, and gave her a deep bow.

"How wonderful. You must sing me every one."

"In time, Majesty. Right now, I'd rather dig into a fine bowl of rabbit stew."

Rhynt nodded vigorously. "As could I. Come, then. You'll sing me songs, and I will fill you in on the various missions underway."

"Missions?"

"Yes, to Mystrosia, Paudia, and the whole wide world, known and unknown."

Whelan cocked his head. "How curious. I can't wait to hear *everything.*"

Rhynt nodded and turned to the hill tigers. "Mela, Mila, Spook—to me!"

13

Orthor couldn't help sighing when he reached the opening to Randall's Cave. Not only was he right back where he started, but he was in a cave that offered stringy rats instead of the plump rats that called The Cave of the Six Arrows their home.

The sun was already setting, so he busied himself with what must be done first: unpack the horses, feed them, water them, and let them loose in the small corral he had built in the first days of his time in Paudia. Then he had carried, sometimes dragged, his supplies: parchments, inks, a bedroll, and a small vessel containing a dozen large snails he hoped would serve as a fixative for his inks, giving them the ability to shrug off water, leaving each message as he had intended it.

It wasn't long before he was sitting beside a small cooking fire, roasting three cave rats on a spit. He tried not to breathe too deeply. The smell of these rats was almost as bad as their taste.

As the rats sizzled, he considered his plan of attack on the runes. Orientation seemed to be key to their understanding. He needed to solve that riddle before he could fully understand the meaning of the drawings in The Cave of the Six Arrows. Why were the gods standing like that, in a circle? What were they standing on? It seemed to be a flat stone, or maybe a platform. Was there significance to the order in which they stood? Were the colors important? And of utmost importance to Queen Rhynt, was the image of the girl who looked like her actually intended to be her? If so, was it a picture that represented the past, the present, or the future? Are those hill tigers Mela, Mila, and Spook? Why were the four of them racing headlong toward the precipice? What was the precipice? The hint of the canyon seemed to suggest the canyon here, but was it?

There were plants along the edge of the cliff, but they were unlike any plant Orthor had ever seen, in person or in a book. Was this, then, a scene from another land?

Orthor sighed. So much to do. He turned his back to the fire, the warmth quickly easing the pain in his back, and watched the last rays of the sun disappear into darkness.

He turned back around and pulled the first sizzling rat from the spit, bouncing it from hand to hand until it was cool enough to bite into. He ignored the taste and had his fill, then banked the fire for the night, the once leaping flames now glowing embers.

He would sleep now. A long day of rune study lay ahead, perhaps more than days, perhaps more than a lifetime. He stood, walked over to his bedroll and eased himself down.

The darkness took him, pulling him into a dream.

Part 3

Sometimes I cannot help but laugh at the hubris of men—or queens. Rhynt's victory is but days old, and already my plan unfolds as I foresaw it, foreordained it. Yes, yes, I admit that the fool's gambit took me by surprise, but it was only a delay. Their surprise victory will ultimately end in a crushing defeat, the queen herself racing unknowingly to her death in a foreign land. What, you still object? Consider where we are, sir. The Mystrosian fleet all but destroyed, Phendour and Blusk marooned on a dead volcano, your hero Calax and that ugly man Marthe about to be drowned, and Rhynt's only allies, the elves, even now sailing away from Enturia in that silly tower, leaving her defenseless. And we have yet to see the mischief to come from my fellow gods Abo, Canto, Dado, and Indo.

Sit now by the fire and watch my plan unfold. I tell you, it will be as exquisite as the wine.

14

Months had passed since Priss and the others had entered the tower. She knew from the rolling effect of the waves that they were still in the great sea, on a two-day trip in outside time to Paudia.

All of them had taken advantage of the extra time that Tower Time had given them. Priss had been able to train her couriers in self-defense, horse-riding, and archery, and was now schooling them on the fine art of archery on horseback, something they'd have to master to be an effective courier in the wilds of Paudia.

Zyrx, proud as he was of his skills as a master blacksmith and armorer, had selected and trained an elf to become master blacksmith of the elves. In his spare time, which was ample, he sat in his room and stared into space, every thought on how to create his fleet of merilium ships.

The Red Monk did as he always did, doing nothing on most days unless called upon. And having not been called upon, he lazed about, took walks in the countryside, gathered mushrooms and flowers for further study as possible medicines, and took full advantage of the elves' hospitality, enjoying more than a few meals with wine each day.

But in the evenings, when the three of them would gather for a late meal and yet more wine, they would sit close and whisper about what they had learned about the elves, the tower, and most important, Queen Daneyh.

The Red Monk was the first to speak tonight. "In my spare time today—"

Zyrx barked out a laugh. "Spare time, spare time, that's all you seem to have!"

The Red Monk frowned at him. "Yeah, yeah, we'll see who has learned the most, then."

"Go on," said Priss. "What did you find out?"

"Nothing definitive," said the Red Monk. "Just another *nuance*."

"Come on," said Zyrx. "What did you find? We don't want to hear about your nuisances."

The Red Monk rolled his eyes. "Nuances, not nuisances. You're the nuisance."

Priss slammed her hand down on the table. "Enough, you two." She glowered at them and they fell silent. "Now, d'Abo, you will tell us what you found." She turned to Zyrx. "And you and I shall listen, yes?"

Zyrx nodded. "Very well."

"All right, then," Priss said, turning to d'Abo. "The floor is yours."

The Red Monk nodded, and leaned in closer to them. "At lunch, I attempted a toast to Queen Daneyh. I was expecting a hearty response, or at least a respectful response, but I was met by silence and strange looks shooting back and forth between the elves. A couple even moved away from me."

"I had a similar experience this morning at breakfast. I did not try to make a toast, but I did ask for toast, and try to engage the young lass who brought it. The mere mention of the queen had her turning on her heels and scurrying away." She looked back and forth at them. "There's something wrong here."

"Aye," said Zyrx. "And the strangest part is that they used to be so joyful before the war with the Mystrosians. The difference is night and day. They seem to be silently oppressed."

"I agree," said Priss, turning to d'Abo. "Is there any way for you to use your powers to dig into this?"

"Yes, that's what I was thinking, too, but there's just one problem: my powers do not work within the tower. I can't send gelas, I can't far-see, I can't affect time, I can't send storms or winds. Nothing works."

Zyrx frowned. "Do you think there's some dark magic at work here, then?"

"I'm not sure yet. The tower is charmed, that's for sure, but the source of the charm, and the extent of the charm, is unclear."

Priss sighed. "I wish Phendour and Blusk were here. They were there when Rhynt supposedly broke the curse, allowing the elves to leave the tower whenever they wanted."

"Yes," said Zyrx. "The witch."

The Red Monk nodded. "Rhynt asked us to learn more about that witch, if we could, so let's do that."

"Right," said Priss. "I'll ask around."

"But don't be direct with them," said Zyrx. "More circumspect— hints, the casual mention, and so on."

"And I'll try to engage the queen directly, in much the same way," said d'Abo.

"Sounds good," said Priss.

The tower rolled sharply. "Oof," said Zyrx, barely catching himself from falling from his chair. "I wish we were on land."

"Aye," said Priss. "Sounds like quite a storm out there."

15

Calax Halfhand stood at the rail of the good ship *Marthe* and looked back and forth between the fast approaching storm behind them and the slow-approaching land in front of them. *Couldn't* Marthe *make this ship go faster?*

Marthe could see Calax's concern. "No worries, Calax. While we go straight for the shore, the storm slants slightly away. It will be a glancing blow. Hard on the ship, but we'll make it." He pointed to the land, a mountainous land with tall trees that swayed in the gusts of wind that had already reached the shore. "There, a harbor of some sort. We just need to scoot in there, and we'll be fine." He looked back at the storm. "We'll make it, just."

Calax looked back at the storm. "I hope you're right." And then at the little harbor and the surrounding land. "Seems to be a caldera. Bad news for anyone who lived here, but good news for us—I hope."

"Aye," said Marthe. He looked at the mountains and the trees and the apparent shape of the island—a crescent. "I wonder."

"What?"

"If this be the legendary land of Mercadia."

"Ha!" said Calax. "How sweet would that be? The queen sends us to find foreign lands and a storm pushes us here. If this truly is Mercadia, the queen will be very pleased."

Marthe shook his head. "From the stories I've heard, I hope it is anything but Mercadia."

Calax looked puzzled. "Why's that?

"The legend, man, the legend."

"That they were a seafaring nation with an unbeatable navy. Yes, I've heard that."

"Not that."

"Then what?"

"The monster, Calax, the monster."

Calax laughed. "Don't tell me you believe in that fairytale. The *Mercadoo*, really?"

Marthe nodded. "I know I am perhaps the ugliest man to ever live, but the Mercadoo was said to be uglier."

"Yes, yes, massive, with long teeth and tentacles, a taste for human flesh, and a roar that could rattle the teeth out of your mouth."

"Exactly," said Marthe. "There are songs about it."

"Pah, *songs*. The minstrels puff up everything. Exaggerate their exaggerations. Let me tell you something, Marthe. If the minstrels were right, I'd be eight feet tall and breathe fire. No, this Mercadoo is a myth and nothing more."

Marthe looked at the island. "Still . . ."

Calax laughed again. "Oh, come on, Marthe. The last person you should believe is a minstrel."

Marthe nodded. "Maybe. But monster or no, we're here." The ship was gliding into the safety of the volcano-created harbor, followed by the other ships. "I better see to the sails."

"Yes, do that." He grabbed Marthe by the arm. "We'll stay here overnight, have ourselves an explore in the morning—it would be great to renew our fresh water stores—and then sail on."

"Very good," said Marthe. He moved away, shouting orders to the sailors to strike the sails and drop anchor.

A nearby clap of thunder startled everyone.

Curious, thought Calax. *I saw no lightning.*

16

Whelan watched Queen Rhynt carefully as they sat alone at the large counsel table. Mela, Mila, and Spook were in their usual places a few strides away, sprawled out in front of the roaring hearth.

The conversation had gone well from Whelan's perspective, Rhynt telling him everything. He already knew most of it and had set his own counterplans in motion. What had surprised him was the mention of an elven queen named Daneyh. He knew the name well, but the Queen Daneyh he knew had been dead for more than five hundred years, killed in a battle on the plains of Paudia, when the elves ruled the land.

But the Daneyh that Whelan had known and counseled was exactly as Rhynt had described her, except for the advice she had given Rhynt. That advice was masterful and far above the actual Queen Rhynt's capacity for reasoned thought or argument. *No*, thought Whelan, *this can only be the witch herself.*

"Tell me again, Majesty, what she said about Paudia."

Rhynt sighed. She was tired, worn out by the stresses of the battle and the decisions she had made since. "She proposed—and I agreed—that the elves set up posts at key locations to prevent an invasion by Ichthia, Olasia, Alamaria, or even the much-weakened Mystrosians."

Whelan shook his head. "Majesty, as a minstrel, I have had the pleasure, or at least the opportunity, to visit all those countries and talk with their kings and queens. None would wish Paudia to be anything but the free lands. Establishing military posts won't prevent invasion; it will provoke invasions."

Rhynt raised an eyebrow. "Provoke?"

Whelan cocked his head. "Yes, Majesty."

"I do not understand."

"Look at your hearth and the roaring fire, Majesty. Now imagine the hearth is Paudia. For hundreds of years it has been without a fire. Its people are free and all that arrive are free also, no matter their crimes elsewhere. It is a land for fresh starts, recuperation from battle—"

"Yes, yes, I see your point," said Rhynt. "And the proposed new posts are the wood that begs to be lit by the Ichthians, the Alamarians, the Olasians, or the Mystrosians. Do I not read you correctly?"

"Indeed you do, Majesty. It will only take a match to set the country ablaze."

"But you said no one wants Paudia to be anything other than Paudia."

"That is true. It is also true that if those countries see this Queen Daneyh and her elves making motions to take over Paudia, they are likely to attack. Not to take over Paudia, but to free her once more."

"So you see those countries as allies of Paudia, and Queen Rhynt as . . ."

"As a threat to Paudia. If you ask me, she is invading Paudia in slow motion. Worse, she is doing it with your knowledge and acquiescence."

Rhynt crossed her arms. *Could this possibly be true? Was she being manipulated by the elf queen? Could the elves who had helped them win the battle against the Mystrosians now be the enemy of Enturia and Paudia and all the rest? And if that's true, what dangers do Zyrx, Priss, and d'Abo face within the tower? By the gods, what have I done?*

She took a deep breath. "What must we do?"

Whelan smiled and reached over to touch her hand. "Don't worry, my dear, I have an idea."

17

Phendour sat on a rock, watching the sun rise on calmer seas, Blusk at her side, grunting over and over again.

"What is it, Blusk?"

"What?"

"The grunting."

"Ah, that would be me thinking, a'course."

"And thought requires annoying grunts?"

Blusk rubbed a hand over his face. "Aye, I mean no, but it helps me think."

"And your thoughts would be?"

"That we are doomed, a'course. Shipwrecked with no hope of survival."

Phendour chuckled and waved her hand over the scene: men scurrying about, unloading supplies from the ship, whose prow pointed toward the sky, a gaping hole in its side. "I see you are taking *all this* well."

Blusk sighed. "Don't make fun of me, Phendour. I'm in no mood."

"I can see that. Now, let's assess our *true* predicament."

"I think I've already covered that. We're as good as done for."

"Not at all, Blusk. Look over there. Do you see them?"

Blusk looked over at the ship, or what was left of it. "Supplies, yes, I'll grant you that, but very little fresh water. Most of the barrels lost in the storm. How's that supposed to make me feel better."

Phendour threw up her hands. Do you not see the men unloading the longboat?"

Blusk's eyes went wide. "By the gods!"

"Or the fates, Blusk. Yes, we have a boat. Now all we have to do is rig a sail, load it with supplies, and be on our way."

Blusk couldn't keep his eyes off the boat. "But which way do we sail?"

"North, of course," said Phendour. "You forget that I was born here on Didu and—"

"Wait, what, this is Didu?"

"Indeed, and if memory serves, we are precisely three hundred miles south of Paudia."

Blusk looked crestfallen. "Three hundred miles? We'll never make it that far."

"Of course we will."

"But we don't have enough water."

Phendour reached over and slapped him on the knee. "Of course we do, you big fool. Didu is much changed since I lived here, but it has not changed entirely. If I'm not mistaken, there's a stream just over that ridge. We only need to find or make enough barrels to see us through."

"Ha! Yesterday you said there was a village *just over the hill*, and there was none."

Phendour nodded. It was true. Strangely true. Buried, no doubt, in lava and ash. "There will be water."

Blusk rolled his eyes. "Okay, let's say that's true. And let's also say we can build enough barrels to hold it. How long will it take us?"

"To reach Paudia?"

"Aye."

Phendour looked out to sea. "Best case, we'll reach Paudia's shores due north in two weeks."

"And worst?"

Phendour didn't want to say. The worst case was that the strong west-to-east current would take them beyond Paudia and even

Enturia into the unknown sea. "Another week, perhaps, dropping us off on the southeast coast."

"Of Paudia?"

"Of Paudia."

Blusk looked out to sea, then back at Phendour. "Let's find some barrels."

18

Queen Daneyh rolled her eyes. This supposed monk was just being insufferable. So many questions. There was no place for such impertinence. *The gall of the man!*

"Stop right there, d'Abo. Once again you miss the point. All of this, all of these . . . *preparations* are known to your queen and are done at her behest."

The Red Monk scowled. "Continuing to make armor, swords, shields, and pikes is far from Queen Rhynt's wishes. She wishes nothing but peace, and she would surely not wish to see Paudia an armed state."

Queen Daneyh clucked. "Nor would I, d'Abo. Nor would I. What we are doing is preparing to defend Paudia from those countries that would take advantage."

The Red Monk crossed his arms and grunted. "I don't see it that way. I see conquest in your eyes."

Queen Daneyh sighed. "Let's just talk a moment about my eyes and what they see ahead for you. You seek to set up a courier system to inform your queen on the progress of that silly little boy and his runes."

"Yes, so?"

"Imagine trying to do that with the armies of Olasia and Ichthia marauding across Paudia."

"Pah," said the Red Monk. "They would not dare. Every country wants Paudia to be a free and peaceful land, to serve as a refuge for scoundrels and a buffer against their enemies."

Queen Daneyh laughed. "Your thinking is behind the times. Once Enturia neutralized Mystrosia, Paudia became up for grabs."

"Nonsense," said d'Abo. "Olasia and Ichthia hate each other and have been at war with each other for centuries. Both see Paudia as a source of sellswords, nothing more."

"You're forgetting one thing: merilium. News has already spread far and wide about its strength. And where, d'Abo, is its source?"

"It's source? What are you talking about? You can't just dig merilium out of the ground. It must be forged from several metals."

"The Olasians and the Ichthians don't know what they don't know. They think they can dig it out of the ground. Think about it, d'Abo. If you were Ichthia or Olasia and had a chance to control a metal that could be the difference maker in your war, wouldn't you attack Paudia?"

The Red Monk sighed. She had a point. "Aye, maybe, but I still don't like these plans of yours."

"Not my plans, d'Abo. *Rhynt's* plan."

"I doubt that, too, Majesty. More like your words in a naïve ear. Rhynt is a wonderful queen, but she is young, with much to learn about the world—and people."

Queen Rhynt cocked her head, and smiled. It was a smile that a cat might have after it had caught and eaten a mouse.

19

Calax was relieved to see the rest of his small fleet of ships safely in the small harbor provided by this caldera of tall mountains and lush forests. From his position at the bow of the good ship *Marthe*, he could also see the remains of structures: ivy covered buildings, a castle, and bridges.

"It is quite a sight," said Marthe.

"Aye," said Calax. "It appears the storm has forced us upon our first discovery for our queen. This was once a proud land. Just look at the magnificence of that castle over there. Even in its current state, it is grander than I have seen anywhere in the known lands."

"No question. I've had a good look at the entire world, and there's nothing grander than this. I wonder what happened."

Calax pointed out at the harbor. "This can be nothing but a caldera, the remains of a once grand volcano."

"Aye. Do you suppose anyone survived?"

"No. It's all so overgrown, I doubt it. More like they fled if they could, and died at sea or somehow made it to other lands. Perhaps even lands that we will yet discover for Queen Rhynt."

"Still . . ."

"What?" said Calax.

"I heard a sound in the night. Not thunder. An animal sound of some sort. Somewhere between a scream and a growl. And loud. So loud."

Calax shook his head. "I heard nothing."

Marthe chuckled. "No, not the way you sleep. And not your snore by the way." He looked up at the mountain and the old castle atop it. "It came from up there."

"Well, then, let's have a look." He glanced at the blue skies. "Weather's good. A fine morning for a walk."

"Aye," said Marthe, "and if there's animals, there'll be water."

"And perhaps people. Make sure the search parties are armed with more than empty barrels."

Bedo, the Green God, watched from the crumbling remains of the castle. His storm had failed, but perhaps the result was even better. Calax had no idea what he was walking into, not at all. *Whelan will be so pleased*, he thought.

20

Orthor moved from rune to rune, studying each from every angle possible, and still the solution eluded him. From one angle, a series of runes seemed to say, "Not the rat," and from another angle, "Build a moat."

"So frustrating," Orthor said to no one. When had he begun to talk to himself? He didn't know and didn't care. "Where's the key?"

He had been up for hours, as usual, checking on how the sun rose on the runes, hoping there would be a new *ah-ha* moment, but the sun held onto its secrets. Only hunger had pulled him away from the runes, Orthor taking just enough time to heat up a leftover rat and make himself a root flour pancake an inch thick.

The rat had gone down easily, even for a stringy rat from Randall's Cave, but he lingered on the pancake, carrying it around and nibbling at its edges as he moved from rune to rune.

A combination of runes caught his attention. Had he seen them before? Where? He ran his fingers over them. He didn't know why, but there was just something about them. "What are you saying?"

The runes stared back. And Orthor didn't have a clue. Frustrated, he slammed his pancake up against the runes and threw it back toward the fire. "I'll just eat another rat. Pancakes are too bitter, anyway."

He sighed and turned back to the runes. Their mystery was apparently safe with him. "By the gods!"

He stormed away from the runes and plopped down next to the fire. He looked back at the runes. "Damn you, damn you all."

He poked the fire hard with a stick, coaxing it back to life. As he leaned forward, trying to strike even harder, his knee touched something cold and soft.

He looked down and picked up the pancake. "You!" He started to throw it toward the mouth of the cave, but stopped and held the pancake up to the light. An impression of the runes on the wall stared back at him. It only took a second for him to see what he had been missing. "*Depth!*"

He raced back to the runes. "It says, "Mercadia, *Mercadia!*"

A lone cave rat scurried away, more impressed by the shout than the discovery.

21

The White Monk, d'Porto Saleen, stood at the prow of the longboat, looking ahead, not behind. He knew if he just turned around, the sight he would see was a soaking wet King Merek the Mighty. *The mighty?* He thought. *More like the pathetic.* The king had been the last to be pulled into the boat, squealing like a little girl.

The last six of his concubines embraced him anyway, warming him with their bodies, which d'Porto had to admit were very accomplished in that area. He glanced back at them. Now they were all huddled around the king, stroking him, kissing him, legs and arms intertwined, looking like a basket of snakes.

He turned back and groaned. Last night's storm had been unforgiving, all the ships shattered and sunk by the wind and waves. But now the sea was calm, without even a puff of wind.

"Where are we?" said the king.

The White Monk thought to ignore him, but kings were kings, after all, so he turned and walked gingerly to the stern of the boat. "I have no idea, Majesty."

"No idea?" What kind of monk are you. "Can't you far-see or something to get our bearings."

The White Monk smirked. "I have already done that, Majesty, to no avail. We are in the middle of the South Sea, somewhere between Paudia to the north and Dido to the south." He pointed to the east. "And we are caught up in a strong current forcing us east."

King Merek's eyes went wide. "East? Back to Enturia?"

The White Monk shook his head. "No, majesty. The current is actually northeasterly. Without any wind, we should come ashore somewhere on the southern coast of Paudia."

"Well, do something about the wind, then."

"I have tried, Majesty, but it appears someone else, someone stronger, won't let me."

"By the gods!"

"Exactly," said d'Porto.

He turned on his heels, leaving a drop-jawed king trying to think of something to say.

The gods, indeed, he thought. *What are they up to now? And where's my White God?*

22

The sail wasn't worth troll shite. It just hung there, doing nothing. No wind. Just the unrelenting current tugging them farther east.

Phendour lifted the bottom of the sail, trying to make it billow, if only a little.

"Don't waste your time," said Blusk. "The gods don't want to give us wind."

Phendour looked at the clouds, the sea, and the horizon. Nothing seemed to indicate a change of weather. "Apparently." She sat down on a rowing bench opposite him. "At least we have water."

"Aye, your little stream was right where you said it would be."

Phendour shook her head. "It was strange being there, on Dido. I haven't seen it in years upon years."

"It looks like it was once a beautiful place."

Phendour attempted a smile. "It was. It was paradise to me. I had no thought of the life I now lead. Back then, I was keen on fishing and farming." She chuckled. "Now look at me."

"Aye, I am, and I see a right amazing archer, sellsword, and warrior—the finest I've known."

Phendour cocked her head. "You know, I've been thinking. I've had enough of this life. I'm thinking once we get to Paudia, I'll turn to farming again. Find a little place to call home and sit there till I die."

Blusk slapped his knee and guffawed. "You, a farmer! No, that will not do."

"I tell you, Blusk, I'm *finished.* "That last battle. I was afraid for the first time in years."

Blusk frowned. "Afraid? You?"

She nodded.

"Well, I don't see you as a farmer. No, not even a little bit."

The sail suddenly stirred, then caught a fresh wind, and billowed.

"Yes," cried Phendour. "Yes!"

She repositioned the sail, and the little boat turned north. "If we can keep this wind, we'll be in Paudia by morning."

"Wonderful," said Blusk. "A right fine wind for sailors—and farmers."

23

Calax ordered four teams of eight men each to search for water on the caldera. One team would proceed west and one team would proceed east along the shore and into the fringes of the jungle, and two teams would spread out and explore the castle and the interior of the island. Any team finding water was to shout out.

Calax led the team into the castle and its surrounds. There was a moat, but the water in it was green with algae, so they passed it by. If all else failed, they could come back for it. The castle itself still maintained much of its grandeur. In fact, Calax thought it much more beautiful than Rhynt's castle. The rooms on the lower floor were larger, as were the abandoned hearths, and the floors were made of brightly painted tiles depicting armies and beasts.

A wide, grand staircase took them to the second level, where the rooms were equally large, but more practical: small hearths and plain stone floors. Pigeons had taken over the high windows, leaving streaks of guano up and down the walls and onto the floor.

They moved on to the royal chambers and were not surprised to see how lavish they were. Bright tiles, large windows, and tapestries beyond compare, though they had faded somewhat over the years.

And then they saw the king's—or perhaps it was the queen's—bed, which was large enough to make a raft that would hold twenty men in full armor and their horses.

They stopped short as they approached it. A dismembered body lay upon it. All dismembered bones now, but judging from the crown that still ringed its decapitated skull, a king or queen had met their fate here. Dried blood was everywhere: on the bed, the floor, and the walls.

Calax took a step closer. These . . . *bones* had once been a proud king. A sword was still in his hand, but had not served him well.

"What beast did this?" said Calax.

They had little time to ponder the answer, because a faraway shout turned their attention back to their goal. "Water, ho!"

"Come on," said Calax. "We'll come back if we have time."

They turned away from the king's bed and made their way back down the stairs, across the moat, and into the jungle. The shouts seemed to be coming from deep in the interior of the island.

"Watch yourselves," said Calax. "Something tore that king apart—something big. It or its children may still live."

They continued into the jungle, each man with his head on a swivel, looking left, right, and all around. The world seemed to grow dark as the jungle enveloped them.

Part 4

All goes well, except for things that don't go well. That is to be expected, of course—humans often turn right when you want them to go left. Yes, Orthor is a problem. He grows closer to a solution. The question for me—for you, for anyone—is how to handle bad news if it comes.

Or rather, when it comes.

News of all kinds is now spreading throughout the known world. Some of it is true—the Mystrosians have been defeated and so on— and some of it is not news at all, mere fabrications by my gods.

I like a good blend of news, true and false, to stir the pot. Don't you?

Now, wipe that scowl off your face and sit by my fire. There is much still to come, and the orchestra tunes its instruments. To your seat!

24

Pandine the Third, King of Kings, Supreme Leader of Ichthia and All He Surveys sat on his throne as he always did on Days of Right and Woe, those days set aside for his people to air their grievances on any and all subjects. His job was to decide all such grievances, from murders to missing goats.

The morning had proceeded well. Even a goat had been returned to its rightful owner. Only four people stood in line, waiting their turn, but Pandine could not keep his eyes off the young woman at the end of the line. She was beautiful. No, she was more than beautiful. She was, she was—he couldn't think of appropriate words. All he knew was that he must have her.

He quickly handled the other grievances, interrupting the grievers halfway through their presentations and quickly reaching the same decision for each—he would give it his consideration on the next Day of Right and Woe. One protested and was dragged away by guards. The other two bowed and bowed again and backed their way from the room.

Leaving the woman. The woman he would have.

He smiled at her. "Come forward, my dear."

She took a step closer and lowered her head. "Yes, Majesty."

Pandine rolled his eyes. "Come now, my dear."

She took two steps forward and stopped.

Pandine shook his head. "No, my dear, here, in front of me, on this spot."

She saw where he was pointing and quickly moved to the spot and curtsied. "Here, Majesty?"

"Indeed," he said, then turned to the others in the throne room. "These proceedings are at an end. Clear the room." He clapped his hands again and again until everyone had scurried away except two guards by the door. "You, too," he said. "And close the doors behind you."

The guards complied, the sound of the slamming doors echoing around the vast throne room.

"Ah," said Pandine. "Alone at last."

The woman's demeanor changed almost immediately. She began pacing up and down in front of him, sizing him up. "I thought you would have been taller, but you're a short one, aren't you—and fat in the bargain."

Pandine sputtered. *The impertinence of the girl*, he *thought, the insolence!* "How dare you!"

The woman shrugged. "Oh, I dare, all right." She pointed at the floor. "Now, on your knees. Time to give me my due."

Pandine's eyes went wide. "Due, due!" He turned toward the doors. "Guards!"

The woman laughed. "You can shout all you want. They're not coming."

Pandine balled up a fist and shook it at her. "Of course they're coming." He strode to the doors and tried to open them.

"That won't do you any good, and besides, you're wasting my time."

"Time? Time? Who are you?"

The woman smiled at him. "Ah, we finally get to the point. Those who love me—*revere* me, *obey* me—call me Abo, The Red God."

Pandine scoffed. "Ha! Fairy tales. There are no such things as gods—just a trick to keep people in line, to obey without thinking."

"Oh, really?" said Abo. She waved her hand, and Pandine lifted from the ground and rose to the ceiling of the throne room, flailing his arms in terror.

"How's that for a fairy tale?" she said with a laugh.

"Let me down!"

Abo shrugged. "As you wish." She made a motion with her hand, and Pandine slowly dropped to the floor.

Once there, he dropped to his knees. "So it is true. I had no idea. I thought the gods were, were . . ."

"Fairy tales?"

He nodded. "Yes." And then he laughed. "I can't believe it. Gods!" He looked up at Abo. "An actual god, here, in Ichthia."

Abo was growing impatient. "Enough, quiet."

"But I have so many questions," said Pandine.

Abo shook her head. "No. I am here to give you a message—*not* to answer questions."

"A message?"

"Indeed."

"Who sends a god to deliver a message?"

"Think about it."

"Another god?"

"That's a question."

"But—"

"Do you want the message, or not?"

Pandine threw up his hands. "Of course. I think."

"Don't think. Listen. I will only say this once—and without interruption. If you interrupt, I will stop, leaving you with only part of a message."

Pandine tried to calm himself. *A god is talking to me! What message could she possibly have for me?* "Um, as you wish. Please proceed."

"The Enturians have defeated the Mystrosians in armed combat," she began.

Pandine thought to interrupt, but slapped a hand over his mouth. *If this is true, there really is an Enturia. The myth is true.*

"I see this news startles you. At any rate, the Enturians are far more powerful than you." She saw he was about to object. "Silence. Believe me, you could not defeat them in battle, at least not now. You need a metal called merilium to make your swords and armor invincible. More to the point, you need a man, a dwarf named Zyrx to make your armor. And once you have that man and that armor, no one will be able to stop you, including Olasia." She watched his eyes grow wide. "I thought you'd like that."

She pulled out a parchment from beneath her cloak. "This is a map to his home in Paudia. It is called the Hearth on the Hill, and is protected by hill tigers. Don't worry, the tigers are elsewhere, in Enturia, with their new queen, Rhynt. You will have no problem taking him." She handed him the map.

He started to say, "But," but she was gone.

He moved slowly across the room and slumped down on his throne. "Merilium? What the hell is merilium?"

25

Orthor set down his quill and rubbed his eyes. He had been working through the night on the translation of the runes on the wall of Randall's Cave, and his neck was sore from turning to and from the runes. He looked down at his right hand. His index and middle fingers were black from ink, as was the bottom of his forearm. Two scrolls were already filled with stories of the fabled land of Mercadia, and he was halfway through a third.

If the runes were true, Mercadia was a wonderful land filled with wonderful people. The island was not large by the standards of the known world—it was about half the size of what remained of Didu—but its soil was rich, making farming and trade lucrative.

Mercadian ships ruled the seas, not by arms but by a vast network of trade with every land. Their ships brought food and minerals to all the others, while bringing home all the riches and delicacies of the world. Mercadians wanted for nothing. Everything about their culture shouted opulence. Even the lowest farmer had a store of gold for a rainy day that never came.

But then things began to change. Earthquakes became stronger and more frequent, and the volcano that occupied the entire east side of the island began to smoke and spew streams of lava.

They thought nothing of it at first—all the lava floes headed east, into the sea. Their homes were safe. There farmlands were safe, and nothing was interfering with the comings and goings of ships from all over the world.

But then the volcano itself began to rumble. Steam poured from vents along its side, and plumes of ash rose seemingly to the heavens. Their king, Balus III, ordered the evacuation of the island "until such time as the volcano grows cooler."

Most Mercadians made it to a ship and sailed to safety, though the runes do not say to where. A ship's captain described the scene as they departed and fled. "And then, on the horizon, we saw a burst of flame fill the sky in all directions, and minutes later a sound that made us cover our ears and fall to the deck of the ship. Our land, our Mercadia, was gone."

Orthor checked the meaning of the final runes one more time. The captain's message was exactly as Orthor had written it on the scroll.

Orthor scanned the cave, looking for more runes, but there were none. "I'll have to go back to The Cave of the Six Arrows now. There are three times the number of runes there, as well as the strange paintings."

He caught himself talking out loud. "Damn!"

He glanced over at the empty bird cage. If only he had waited. He could have sent a pigeon to the queen with news of Mercadia, including its exact location in the seas far from Enturia's eastern shore.

"Now I'll have to finish up at the other cave and make my way home as quickly as I can manage."

He rolled his eyes. "Talking again. Sorry, cave. Sorry, rats."

He took the finished scrolls across the cave and hid them behind a rock. He would leave them here. If the Red God showed up, she would have no reason to doubt what he would call his lack of progress.

26

Calax and his men were the last to arrive and wonder at the waterfall flowing over the side of the mountain and down into a canyon so deep no man would approach the edge. The stream that fed it was roaring, overflowing its banks from last night's storm.

A man was bent over the stream, about to put his bucket in to collect water. Calax shouted for him to stop, but the man put his bucket in the water and was immediately pulled in and swept over the edge.

Calax turned to the others. "The stream is too strong here. Let's follow it upstream and looked for pools along its sides."

A hundred yards upstream they came upon a pool a man wide and a man deep, the waters in it swirling but much calmer than the main body of the stream. Every man with a bucket dipped it in and began filling the small water barrels they had brought along. An hour later, the men, laden with the thirty barrels of water they had managed to collect, made their way down the mountain and out of the jungle, their ships in sight in the harbor below.

Calax grabbed the man in the lead by the arm. "Take them down and see to the storage of the water. I want to have a look around."

The man nodded and walked away, making sure all the others were following him.

When the last man walked by, Calax turned and headed for the castle. *Who were these people?* He had to know.

27

The tower arrived at Port Ochno, on the eastern shore of Paudia, in the early morning. Mist shrouded the port town, or what was left of it after the Mystrosians had stormed through on their ill-fated attack on Enturia just weeks earlier.

A tiny door opened at the base of the tower, and a group of tiny people and horses rode out, instantly growing in size.

"That always makes me dizzy," said the Red Monk.

"Woo," said Priss. "My first time, but I see what you mean."

"I hope never to get used to it," said Zyrx. "In fact, I hope never to leave the Hearth on the Hill again." He looked around, then pointed through the mist. "Priss, see that hill over there?"

Priss squinted into the distance. "Yes, I think so."

"That's your path, up the hill, across the plain, to the Randall's Cave. Trust the map you've been given."

Priss pulled her horse up alongside Zyrx's, and offered her hand. "May you reach your home without incident. Are you sure you will not accompany us to the caves?"

"No, I have work to do for the queen. The caves would take me too far off my path, but I wish you a safe journey. With any luck, Orthor will have already finished his work and you'll be right back here in a few days, waiting for transport back to Enturia."

"I hope you're right," said the Red Monk, riding up beside them. "Come, Priss, we need to make the most of daylight. We've a two-day ride ahead of us." He turned to Zyrx. "Farewell, my friend. I hope we meet again down the road."

Zyrx chuckled. "Oh, you'll see me again. I promise you that, but not for a time. Gods speed to you."

The Red Monk nodded and rode off to join the men, women, girls, and boys who had been selected to serve as couriers bringing messages to and from Orthor and the queen.

"Farewell, Zyrx." She gave him a big smile, then turned her horse and galloped off.

Zyrx watched them until they had disappeared over the hill, then turned his horse and the packhorse that trailed it to the west. "Come along, horsie, we have miles to go this day and three more if memory serves."

Had he stayed a few minutes longer, he would have seen hundreds upon hundreds of armed elves on horseback pouring from the tower, heading in all directions.

28

The southern coast of Paudia appeared first as a dark, wavy line across the horizon, a line that grew thicker, with touches of greens and yellows before becoming recognizable as land itself.

Everyone on Phendour's and Blusk's longboat held their collective breaths on the slow approach, worrying that the boat may come close, but then be swept past Paudia and into The Great Sea.

Finally, Phendour let out a shout. "We're going to land!"

"Where?" said Blusk.

"About two hundred yards further east." She turned to the others. Watch the depth. As soon as it reaches waist deep, we need to jump out and push her to shore. Get ready."

Phendour looked over the side and watched as the deep greens of the sea grew paler and clearer, slowly revealing the sandy bottom. She looked at the shore. There was no doubt now that they were slanting in toward the beach. "Get her ashore," she shouted, jumping over the side. The shock of the cool water made her shout again. "Come on, we've made it."

The others soon joined her, some jumping in reluctantly, others squealing like children as they leaped into the water.

Blusk came last, the most reluctant. "I can't swim!"

"It's only knee deep now," said Phendour. "You can stand."

Blusk closed his eyes and jumped, his splash nearly pushing the longboat back out to sea.

"By the gods," said Phendour, grabbing the side of the boat and tugging it toward shore. "You nearly sunk us."

Blusk said nothing as he rushed through the water to the beach, where he collapsed to his knees. "You nearly drowned me."

Phendour and the others ignored him. With one final great effort, they pushed and tugged the longboat ashore, securing it to the beach by tying it off on a boulder.

Phendour looked up and down the shore. There was nothing in sight. Then she spotted a column of smoke far off to the north. "Looks like a fire, maybe a tavern if we're lucky." She turned to the men. "Let's get the supplies from the boat and head inland. We don't want to be here when the tide comes in."

"Will the longboat be safe?" said Blusk.

Phendour shrugged. "Once we have the supplies, I couldn't care less. We're in Paudia now. The next ship we see will be in Port Ochno."

"How far do you figure?"

Phendour shook her head. "By the look of the land, we're at least sixty miles away. It will be quite a walk."

"Aye. Well, let's hope that smoke is a tavern. Right about now I could eat the worst mutton in the known world."

Phendour smiled and looked at the other men. "As could we all."

"Let's go, then," said Blusk. "We're losing light."

Phendour waved for the others to join them and began trudging north toward the rising smoke.

29

Abo, the Red God, was tired of playing games. There would be no pretense that she was a supplicant seeking relief from some imagined hurt. No, she would catch him while he was alone and unattended. The best place for that was the king's bed, or at least beside it.

She reached out and nudged his shoulder. "Wake up."

King Wazapor IV, Esteemed Ruler of Olasia, Legendary Snorer, swatted at her hand and rolled away to the other side of the bed.

Abo rolled her eyes. "This will not do." She raised her hand and mumbled a single word, and the king rolled back to her and opened his eyes, which grew wider and wider as sleep left him and a look of wonder took over his face. "Oh, my, are you the new concubine?"

She frowned. "Hardly. No, I am here to give you a message."

The king was persistent. "But you are so beautiful. You *must* be the new concubine."

"No, I am Abo, the Red God, and you best listen."

He seemed not to hear her. "Oh, *please* be my new concubine."

Abo reached down and grabbed him by the throat, the king grabbing her arm with both hands, struggling to wrestle free, but she held him firm. "You color well when you're strangled. A wonderful red, like a dolo melon. You should see it."

The king grunted, his eyes bulging.

She shook her head and released him. "But you have ugly black eyes."

King Wazapor gasped for breath and rubbed at his neck. "What . . . what do you want?"

Abo sighed. What a stupid man. "As I have already said, I am here to give you a message."

He started to interrupt, but she held up her hand. "No, I am tired of interruptions. Put your hand over your mouth and open those big flapping ears of yours."

He complied without a word, and she delivered the message, every word reflected in the movement of his black eyes. There was surprise there, and greed, and opportunity, and delight.

30

Calax made his way back to the castle and climbed the stairs to the king's bedroom. He examined the bones again, lifting each bone or piece of bone and its place in or around the bed. Whatever had killed him was not just powerful, but impossibly powerful. Bones had not just been severed, but in several cases crushed to powder.

He looked at the walls closest to the bed. Blood had sprayed over twenty feet, indicating the ferocity of the attack. And more blood was even farther away from the bed, as if the beast had shaken his head to rid himself of the blood.

He looked at the windows high above the bed. Too small for a beast with such power. Then he turned and looked at the double doors, both of which had been ruptured from their hinges. If he was right, the beast was at least eight feet tall and equally wide. *No such thing,* he thought.

A nursery rhyme suddenly popped into his head.

To bed, my child, the night grows nigh
To bed, my love, the beast screams high
To bed, go now, my story is true
Don't be a meal for the Mercadoo

Calax couldn't help smiling. His mother had sung that to him every night when he was a child. And when she reached the last line, she would tickle him. It was all a game, and not very effective. When she left the room, he had immediately jumped out of bed and continued playing.

And then he frowned. Could this island really be the remains of the mythical Mercadia, and could that monster possibly be real? He shook off the thought. *Ridiculous!*

But still.

He walked around the room, looking for any sign that would identify the name of the king or this strange land, but he found nothing. The other rooms on the king's landing, mainly apartments for his attendants and a large room for his concubines, revealed nothing except a singular question: *why was the king alone here? Where were the other people?*

Nothing indicated rapid flight from a beast. Save for years of dust, nothing seemed disturbed. In fact, nothing indicated flight at all. Beds were made. Clothing was neatly folded and stored. Desiccated fruit filled bowl after bowl. And yet the people had vanished.

Calax walked downstairs and found similar scenes: a pristine throne room, a kitchen in perfect order, hearths filled with wood, ready for a fire.

He continued downward, taking a spiral staircase down to what must have been a dungeon. With each step, the air grew colder. At the bottom of the staircase, the room opened up to a large room filled with barrel after barrel of shriveled up fruit and potatoes that had once been the size of his head. Cold storage, he thought. They didn't want for anything.

A door at the far end of the room caught his attention. Opening it, he discovered another staircase, spiraling into the darkness. He walked back across the room and up the spiral staircase to the kitchen, where he found a torch and a flint to help him light it.

Moments later, he was back at the door to the second staircase. He held the torch in front of him and walked slowly down the stairs to a landing and a long hall with barred cells on either side. Ten in all.

He held up the torch as he examined them. Nothing out of order. No prisoners. No skeletons. Nothing.

And then a sound erupted from somewhere deeper in the castle. A growl, guttural and deep. *And aware.*

Calax spotted the next staircase and drew his sword.

31

The trip from Randall's Cave to the Cave of the Six Arrows had taken longer than expected, thanks to Orthor's decision to move everything there. He had done as much as he could at Randall's Cave, so moving all his things made sense. Still, the packing, the trip, and the unpacking, including dealing with the needs of the horses, had left him exhausted.

He should have immediately set to work translating the runes and interpreting the cave paintings, but he thought a fine rest at a warm fire with a sizzling hot and succulent cave rat seemed the better choice. One cave rat had led to a second and a third, and he had then fallen into a deep sleep.

In his dream, he was back in Enturia, talking with the Librarian about his exploits in the caves.

"You would have hated it, sir, especially the rats in Randall's Cave."

"Indeed, I would. You actually ate rats?"

"Oh, yes, though the ones in the Cave of the Six Arrows were far superior. A taste similar to rabbit and molfrump, but less gamey."

"I will take your word for it. Now, as I am busy with this and that, please let me know why you are here, and for which and for what."

"Oh, I thought you knew. I have translated the runes in both caves. Amazing stuff, really, and—"

"But why are you here, *now?*"

"Oh, of course. The runes mentioned several scrolls and books. I'm hoping to find copies here."

"Well, out with it, boy. Which scrolls and books?"

"Mellon's *Mercadian Myths and More!*, as well as Sellwynn's *Monsters of the Known World* and Capusetta's *Rhymes for the Nursery.*"

"Hmm. I don't remember ever seeing those here. Are you sure you have the titles right?"

"Yes, of course. The runes were very specific."

"Well, then, you can ignore the Hall of Scrolls and the Book Stacks."

"But what—"

"As well as the Classification and Sorting Room."

"But—"

"No, I'm afraid you will have to start with the Pile of Loose Pages and Damaged Scrolls."

Orthor awoke screaming. "By the gods!"

The memory of the Pile of Loose Pages and Damaged Scrolls sent shivers up his spine. That had been his first assignment, sifting through the loose and damaged documents for hidden treasures. Mostly it was a thankless, frustrating task, but he had been able to find all but three pages of Grantnod's Peasant Cookery, Fifth Edition. The Librarian had been particularly effusive when he discovered that Orthor had found the recipe for Molfrump Marinade, a sauce said to be approaching magical in its ability to tenderize the meat.

Orthor poked at the fire and threw another log on, the cave growing brighter, the runes almost sparkling, the paintings beckoning him to get to work. Is that Queen Rhynt running toward the abyss with her hill tigers? And if so, when? And why?

He sighed and looked around for another rat.

32

The fire snapped and crackled, pale smoke rising through the canopy of trees where the White Monk and King Merek and his concubines had settled down for the night. Even in the dim light provided by the small fire, it was easy to see that these reluctant travelers had been through an ordeal.

The White Monk's normally brilliant white robes and cowl were now stained by the sea and the long walk into the plains of Paudia. His robes were beige up to the knee and a rope of seaweed curled around his left leg.

The king was no better. His splendid velvet tunic and robes had been ruined, the velvet now looking like stalks of wheat that had been flattened by a strong wind.

And his concubines, more beautiful than most women in the known world, looked like peasants in rags, their translucent clothing, no thicker than a molfrump hair, torn and wrinkled, their hair going this way and that. And they wouldn't stop whining.

"Majesty," said d'Porto, "can you not get them to be quiet, if only for a minute."

King Merek the Mighty shrugged and tugged at his robe, trying to make it close. "Damnable robe. Look, it's shrunk. And no, the concubines do what they do. If you don't like it, get us the hell out of here with your magic."

The concubines continued whining.

The White Monk stood and paced in front of the fire. "Majesty, Majesty, have you not been listening? I have no powers. For some reason, the White God has abandoned me. I cannot far-see. I cannot send gelas. I cannot even light a fire without the help of flint. I am—"

"A useless man in dirty clothes," said the king. He threw up his hands. "Like me."

The White Monk tried to console him. "Well, at least you have your concubines."

The king laughed. "My concubines? More like sirens, and not as pretty in their soiled clothes."

The concubines whined louder.

The king sighed. "I did not mean that. You are all beautiful, and I adore each and every one of you."

The king stood, grabbed the White Monk by the arm, and pulled him away from the fire. "Come, let's talk."

"About what?"

The king spread his arms. "This! This shithole of a country we find ourselves in. What do we do? How do we get home? *Where* is home?"

The White Monk put his hand on the king's shoulder. "We will know more in the morning, Majesty. The sun rises in the east, as it has always done, so we can take our bearings and head north."

The king frowned. "North? But Mystrosia is west, is it not?"

"Yes, yes, but we must first find the main road, and that is farther inland. Once we find the road, we'll turn west and follow it to Paudia's western port."

"I think not," said a voice from the darkness.

The king and d'Porto startled, but there was nothing they could do. The next second they were surrounded by a dozen warriors.

"No, once we reach the road, we'll be turning right, toward Port Ochno," said Phendour.

"Indeed," said Blusk, "but first we'll build a decent fire."

The king, who should have felt defeat, instead felt overwhelming relief, and cried. The White Monk cringed at the display. And the concubines whined.

33

Priss, Zyrx, and the Red Monk were greatly relieved when they crested the bluff at Port Ochno and made their way across the vast plain between them and Randall's Cave.

The couriers that Priss had picked and trained laughed among themselves as they trotted along trailed by the pack horses and two dozen spare horses. As much as she wanted to join them, Priss had to pay attention to the map and make sure everyone was headed in the right direction, at the right speed. Too fast and they'd exhaust the horses, too slow and they'd arrive at Randall's Cave at night, which was not a good idea—Priss had told everyone about the monster that lurked in the river by the cave.

Everything was going well, except for the Red Monk. He kept pulling up his horse and dropping into a trance. Finally, Priss had trotted back to confront him. "What are you doing? You're slowing us all down."

The Red Monk broke from his trance, and blinked. "What? What did you say?"

"I said, what are you doing?"

"Oh, oh, this. I've been far-seeing, and I don't like what I see. No, I don't *believe* what I'm seeing."

"And that would be?"

"The tower. It's not moving from Port Ochno as we believed. It's doing something strange." He paused and shook his head in disbelief.

"Go on."

"Well, the tower is depositing whole buildings and walls from a door of some sort in its bottom."

"Whole buildings? How is that possible?"

"Come on, Priss, you've seen what they can do, and with the time difference between Tower Time and time in the outside world gives them plenty of time to build."

"So they're rebuilding what the Mystrosians destroyed. What's wrong with that?"

"But now it's much larger than it was, and the whole town is fortified."

Priss shrugged. "But Queen Daneyh said they'd be building fortified outposts."

"Yes, but she said they'd be built in the north, to prevent invasions from Ichthia and Olasia."

Priss frowned. "Perhaps it's just a precaution, a place to fall back on if things don't go well in the north."

"I hope you are right. At any rate, I'll keep an eye on them."

"Do that, but while you're doing that, please keep up with the rest of the column. You're slowing us down. If we don't pick up the pace, we won't make it to the midpoint before sunset."

The Red Monk sighed. "Very well. I'll wait until we get there to far-see again."

"Good," said Priss, turning her horse and galloping back to the front of the column.

The Red Monk looked back in the direction of Port Ochno. "I do not like this."

34

Calax made his way down the staircase, his torch held high and his sword ready to strike. The growling grew louder, and then stopped. Calax paused to listen.

Nothing.

He took a tentative step forward, revealing more of the staircase. A few yards ahead, it turned sharply to the right, and he could see that the stairs there were even steeper. He approached the turn slowly, and then peered down as far as the light allowed. There was a new sound now, the sound of breaking waves. The staircase was leading him outside, somewhere at the base of the castle, or somewhere even deeper, perhaps a water-filled cave leading to a beach.

He heard the snap of a branch and then saw the shape of something big and black hurtling toward him. He raised his sword just in time to strike hard at the beast's belly, and it fell lifeless in front of him. He held up the torch. A black leopard.

And where there's a predator, there's prey, he thought. They had not seen any evidence of animal life on the island, save for the calls of unseen birds deep in the jungle. But the appearance of a leopard suggested an island teeming with life. The only question was, where was it?

He continued down the stairs, which opened to a small, empty room with an open door to the outside. He took a step out and looked in all directions. He was in the jungle, on a cliff that dropped off to the sea below. To his right, there was nothing, but to the left he could see a path holding close to the castle walls.

Calax held his torch high and made his way through the jungle and around the castle to the front. He could see the ships bobbing in the light chop of the harbor. All the men seemed to be aboard.

But they were not going anywhere. Not now. They would stay and explore every inch of this island. There was food here—and a beast of some kind—and he would not leave until he knew everything about this land.

I will send a bird to the queen, he thought. *She must know of this.*

35

Priss was pleased with their progress across the plains of Paudia and on the map she was given, which indicated that they were better than halfway to Randall's Cave. When they came upon a likely spot for a camp, she raised her hand and signaled them to stop.

An hour later, everyone was settled around a fire except for the Red Monk, who stood apart, clearly still in his far-seeing trance. Priss looked back and forth between the monk and the rabbits roasting on a spit not a yard away. When she saw the monk break from his trance, she stood and walked up to him. "What did you see?"

The Red Monk sighed. "It is as I feared. Port Ochno is now a fortified, walled city."

"What of the tower?"

He rolled his eyes. "That's the worst part. It is speeding faster than an arrow down the main road, dropping villages and forts as it goes."

Priss laughed. "Faster than an arrow. Come on, nothing else could go that fast."

The Red Monk puffed out a breath. "And yet it is so. Paudia is being transformed. Walled cities, forts, new villages. Queen Daneyh is not protecting Paudia, she is taking it over. Thousands of elves everywhere, and more coming by the minute."

"But Queen Rhynt said—"

"Yes, I know, but she was taken in by Queen Daneyh's ruse."

"But—"

"But nothing." He grabbed her by the elbow and led her farther from the fire, so no one could overhear. "Our mission is at an end."

Priss's eyes went wide. "What? What are you talking about?"

"There is no way for us to set up a courier system between Orthor and the queen. My guess is the first rider and others that follow would be stopped at Port Ochno and imprisoned—or worse."

"But you don't know that for sure. We dare not disobey the queen."

The Red Monk couldn't help chuckling. "*Disobey?* Priss, there is no way to *obey*. Our best course is to flee."

Priss frowned at him. "No, I will not disobey my queen without proof."

The Red Monk rolled his eyes. "Proof? What proof would satisfy you? I've told you what I saw."

"But I didn't see it. You may have misinterpreted Queen Daneyh's actions."

The Red Monk threw up his hands in frustration. "Priss, Priss, what will satisfy you?"

"I would know what Queen Daneyh's plan is."

"And how would I know that?"

"Can't you find her and send a gela."

The Red Monk started to object. He knew the queen was in Port Ochno, but he wasn't sure he could send and control a gela that far and for long enough to learn anything. But then he nodded. "Yes, perhaps, but it will take everything out of me. Go back to the fire and enjoy your rabbits. I'll send a gela this minute."

"Excellent," said Priss.

She started to leave, but the Red Monk caught her by the arm. "One thing. After this, I will be exhausted to the point of appearing dead. I assure you, I will still be alive. You will need to strap me to my horse and proceed at speed for Randall's Cave. If I am lucky, I will revive by then. And then I hope to tell you her plan. The important thing is to get to the cave as quickly as you can. Elves are spreading across the land in every direction. We simply have to outrun them."

Priss nodded, and the Red Monk let go of her arm. "Go then, enjoy the rabbit. It smells wonderful."

Priss nodded again. "I will do as you say."

"Do not look back or draw attention to me in any way. I may appear to be in a fit to make this work. Let no man interrupt me. It would be my death."

"I will do as you say. Good luck with your task." She turned and walked back to the fire, the scent of the succulent rabbits growing stronger with each step.

She began to drool.

36

Queen Rhynt, Baron Bookins, and Whelan the Wanderer sat at the Queen's End of the long conference table in the council chambers, each lost in their thoughts after more than an hour of discussion. Mela, Mila, and Spook lazed by the fire, which had gone from blazing to embers.

They had talked about Queen Daneyh's advice, about the puzzlement of the two pigeons, and next steps. Whelan thought that they should do nothing, just wait for Priss and the others to set up the courier network. Bookins thought they should send several pigeons to Orthor, each with the same message, to provide an update on his progress. Queen Rhynt agreed with them both, and added another possibility: sending pigeons to Calax and Phendour to seek their advice and to get an update on their missions. In the end, they had agreed to do everything except Whelan's do-nothing suggestion.

Bookins tapped his fingers on the table. "Is there to be wine?"

Queen Rhynt chuckled. "Soon, baron, soon, if they listened well to my instructions, and a fine plate of food as well."

"Ah," said Whelan. "I could eat the much talked about horse. Thinking and talking always make me hungry."

"Aye," said Rhynt.

Bookins smiled at her. "After the meal, I'll see to the pigeons. We only need agree with the messages to be sent."

Whelan sighed. "I'd like to revisit the instructions to Calax and Phendour. As I've said, I think Queen Daneyh was right in this regard. A show of force—and, really, it's only a sail-by—would do no harm, and might do some real good. Make Olasia and Ichthia have second thoughts of taking advantage of the situation."

Bookins puffed out a breath. "Majesty, we have been over this already." He turned to Whelan. "Yes, a sail-by would send that message, but it would also send a second, and I must say, *unintended* message: that we have designs on them and the rest of the known world."

Whelan rolled his eyes. "And what is wrong with them thinking that?"

Queen Rhynt leaned toward him, anger growing in her. "Because that is not my intent, and I'll have none of it. No, Phendour and Blusk must return with their fleet straightaway, as soon as they have delivered the Mystrosians to their shores. And Calax must break off his mission and return immediately. I was wrong to so spread out our armies. They are needed here."

Whelan held up his hands. "As you wish, Majesty. As you wish."

The door to the council chambers opened and several servants walked in carrying trays of food and wine.

Queen Rhynt turned to Bookins. "You and I will craft the messages after our meal." She turned to Whelan. "You can do whatever you wish, Whelan. Write a song, perhaps, lamenting the state of this world."

Whelan chuckled. "Perhaps I shall."

37

Phendour, Blusk, and the other men who had survived the wreck of the flagship tried their best to keep the king, the white monk, and the concubines moving at speed, in the right direction. The concubines moved fastest, and had stopped whining, but the white monk and the king moved as if stuck in mud.

"Why do we have to move so fast," the king moaned. "I just don't understand what the rush is."

"Nor I," said the White Monk.

Blusk pushed them both in the back. "Just move, I'm tired of your whining. First it was your concubines, and now you, the both of you."

"But I'm exhausted," said the king, "and hungry."

Blusk looked up at the sun, and then turned to Phendour. "He has a point. It nears midday. Perhaps we should sup, let them rest their legs."

Phendour knew from the position of the sun that Blusk had a point. They had to stop sometime, so why not now? "Very well, but it leaves us with very little time to make it to the main road before nightfall."

"And why is that even a goal?" said the White Monk, stopping in his tracks and plopping to the ground. "Ah, that's better."

Phendour rolled her eyes, then shouted at the others. "Hold! We stop here."

She turned back to the White Monk. "If I am not mistaken, there is a small inn directly north of here, and I don't want to miss it in the darkness."

The White Monk laughed. "An inn? Don't you realize that if it is anywhere near the main road, it would have been destroyed as we marched across Paudia?"

"That is possible."

"No, that is a certainty."

"You are said to have vast powers, so prove it. Far-see and tell us now what you see."

The White Monk sighed. "Would that I could. My god has deserted me, and taken all my powers with him."

Phendour nodded. "I should have thought of that. Yes, he was killed by one of my archers, a fine young girl named Priss."

The White Monk giggled. "Yes, yes, but that doesn't keep a god down for long. They can't be killed absolutely. From what he told me, they go to a place of darkness, then emerge even stronger than before."

"Hmph."

"Hmph, indeed. So the question, at least for me, is why has he abandoned me, here, in this godawful place, no pun intended?"

Phendour didn't have an answer. "So you will be of little help to us on our journey?"

The White Monk shrugged. "So it seems, at least where magic is concerned. But I have a fine mind, and know things. That should help."

"Know things? What things?"

The White Monk pointed at the horizon. "Well, for starters, those black clouds suggest the storm has found us again. And if I can put this and that together, it suggests to me that the White God is not finished with us. We'd best forget a meal and press on toward that inn of yours."

Phendour looked at the sky. It was as he said. A storm was coming. A big storm.

38

Queen Daneyh came out of her trance smiling. All was going well, in all directions. Port Ochno had been transformed into a heavily fortified, impenetrable city, just as she had demanded it be, complete with a castle for her and her lords. Additional villages and forts were being built and deposited along the main road. In just days of Paudian Time, this once free land would be an armed camp from coast to coast, with thousands upon thousands of warriors defending her.

She had felt strange leaving the tower, but it was easier to far-see and control things here in her new castle. The only question was how and when to deal with Zyrx, Priss, that damnable Red Monk, and the others.

She could send search parties for them right away, but she wanted them to lead her to Randall's Cave. Something important was going on there, apparently, and she wanted to know what it was and how valuable it might be. Delaying their capture would give her time to complete her work on transforming Paudia to what had been thousands of years ago, when elves ruled, a time before the arrival of the witch who had locked them in the tower.

A knock at the door to her chambers drew her attention. "Who is it?"

A voice, muted by the thickness of the door, said, "A guard, your Majesty."

Oh, bother, she thought. "Enter."

The guard opened the door only enough to stick his head into the chamber. "The council awaits you and seeks your presence."

"Is it that time already?"

"Yes, Majesty. Apparently, Majesty."

"Then tell them I will be along presently."

"Yes, Majesty." He clicked his heels and shut the door.

The queen sighed. "I don't know why I agreed to a council. A complete waste of time."

39

Zyrx coaxed his small horse and the trailing packhorse into the cover of a copse of trees along the main road. From the sound of it, something big was coming, and coming fast.

The ground was shaking so much, he thought he was being chased down by a horde of angry trolls.

The first hint of what was coming up behind him was a group of elf warriors on horseback charging down the main on the road. He held the horses steady as they passed, a cloud of dust rising up on the road, leaving Zyrx near blind to what was coming next.

Seconds later, he could see the edges of a structure he knew all too well: the tower, moving high over the road and dropping buildings—*whole buildings!*—into place along both sides of the road.

Both sides? thought Zyrx, pulling on the reins and moving the horses as fast as he could away from the road. What looked like an inn nearly crushed them as it settled into place.

"By the gods! What madness is this?"

He knew the answer to the question. Queen Daneyh was transforming Paudia, making it her own.

He dug his heels into the haunches of his horse again and again to get it moving. "Come on, we must get as far away from this road as we can—*fast!*"

His little horse reared briefly, nearly toppling Zyrx to the ground, and bolted into the forest, the packhorse struggling to keep up and Zyrx struggling to hang on.

A few minutes later, he slowed the pace. They still had a long way to go to reach the Hearth on the Hill, and he didn't want to wear out the horses before he was even halfway home. An hour later, he stopped the horses near a stream and dismounted. They needed to rest, to eat and drink, before going on.

And Zyrx needed to think.

What Queen Daneyh is doing is far more than set up defensive outposts. No, she is conquering Paudia, making it her own.

Another thought felt like a punch to his chest. *And she will be coming for me.*

And then another sobering thought: *And the others!*

40

Orthor had set to work after the third rat, arranging his quills, filling the ink well on his writing rock, and setting out the first suitable parchment. He looked at the runes, and the runes clicked into place. Obscure scribbling became words and sentences and the continuing story of Mercadia and its disastrous end.

Orthor could not write fast enough, his penmanship suffering but still readable as he recorded shock after shock. Mercadia, an island leagues and leagues away from Enturia, was a peaceful kingdom known for its dense jungle, black leopards, and most significant, a volcano that occupied the eastern end of the island.

It had existed for thousands of years, thriving on the export of black leopard skins and a potent liquor made from Anua Fruit and Sanga Root. It was said that the drink could cure all ills, but its main effects were intoxication and hallucination.

One hallucination seemed to be prevalent among all drinkers on the island: a monster that would transform from a beautiful maiden to a hairy beast thick in the chest, with preternaturally long tentacles that could crush a man. It had three eyes, one larger than the other and centered between the two, and a large mouth with two rows of long sharp teeth. Its howl was said to be high-pitched, like the scream of a maiden in danger. That trait was a lure for would-be rescuers, who would rush to the "maiden's" aid and be ripped apart and devoured.

Orthor set down his quill and sighed. *Why would anyone stay in such a place?* He looked back at the runes, and the runes answered.

Two things kept Mercadia's population in place. First, the sudden appearance of the beast was rare, and only at night, and second, all maidens who had reached their red time were required to be locked up and shackled every night.

Orthor set down his quill again. What a terrible time to be a maiden. And how long did they keep this imprisonment up? Till the girls had become crones?

He turned his attention back to the runes, hoping to see a further description of the beast and of Mercadia and its end, but there was a blank section of wall, followed by a description of a conflict between the gods and a demigod, the daughter of a witch and one of the gods, a girl with fiery red hair accompanied by three hill tigers.

Orthor gasped.

Queen Daneyh looked around the table at the elves she had selected to serve on her Council. Not a single one of them was worthy, and not a single one of them was needed. They were all just artifice and façade, their only value creating the semblance of an advisory council. For whatever reason, the populace felt more comfortable knowing that the queen was being advised, that she was being checked in some way. Not that she was.

Oh, yes, she would let them speak, let them spout their weak, sometimes impertinent, ideas, nodding and smiling at them as if their ideas were gold and jewels to be treasured. But even they knew they were playing a game, their words meaningless to the queen. The only thing of importance to the council members was to maintain their positions and the perquisites of office.

Occasionally, a council member would inadvertently say something that displeased the queen, and when that happened, they were never seen again. Their place at the table was filled by another elf elevated seemingly at random by the queen.

The queen cleared her throat. "Thank you once again for your advice. I am always amazed by the ideas presented here and by the dedicated work of this council. Truly, our people owe you praise beyond measure, as do I."

She paused to gauge the reception of her words. Everyone was smiling and nodding, pleased that she was pleased and that they had survived another council meeting—so far.

"Now you see the fruit of your idea for me to pose as a wizard to draw in Rhynt, Calax, Phendour, and Blusk. Rhynt has become queen, yes, but she is weak and naïve. She has sent Calax on a voyage of exploration—ridiculous, but to our advantage. And Phendour and Blusk trained our now invincible army. No one can stand against our skills and our numbers."

She laughed. "And let's not forget about Zyrx, who introduced us to merilium and trained an army of blacksmiths to forge our weapons. We owe them all much."

An elf raised a hand. "But why did we let them go when we landed here? Aren't they a threat to what we're doing?"

Queen Daneyh glowered at him. "A threat? No. No more than a detail, a detail to be dealt with—now." She looked at the elf to her left. "Send forces to capture them all."

"Yes, Majesty."

"And if they resist, kill them."

"Yes, Majesty." The elf stood, bowed to the queen, and left the room.

The queen waited until the door clicked shut before continuing. "Now, let's get back to the schedule. As I understand you, Paudia will be fully in our grasp in two weeks of Outside Time."

They all nodded.

"So let's work toward our first attack. We will need ships, hundreds of ships."

They all nodded, and Queen Daneyh smiled.

42

The Red Monk dropped out of his trance and screamed. "No!"

"What?" said Priss. "What did your gela see?"

He rubbed a hand over his face, trying to shake off the last effects of far-seeing through a gela. "Too much, and enough."

"You speak in riddles. I can tell something is wrong, but what?"

The monk nodded. "There are no riddles here. Queen Daneyh and her warriors have taken over Paudia and mean to conquer the world, using Paudia as their home base. In just weeks, all of Paudia will be an armed camp."

"We must warn Queen Rhynt," said Priss.

The Red Monk agreed, but shook his head nonetheless. "Yes, but I fear they will be intercepted by Daneyh. She is very powerful. More powerful than me, for sure, and perhaps even the Red God."

Priss nodded. "We have thirty birds, so perhaps we can send a half dozen to improve our chances."

"Yes, we will do that, but I'm not sure it will have the desired effect."

"Surely one will get through."

"That's not what I mean. I mean to say that Rhynt has sent Calax and a fleet to explore the world, and Phendour and Blunt to return the Mystrosians to their homeland. All our power is at sea, leaving Enturia in jeopardy from even the smallest attack."

"Did Daneyh mention the target of their planned attack? Perhaps she's thinking of attacking Olasia or Ichthia."

"No, she didn't say, but Enturia seems the most likely to me."

"I disagree," said Priss. "Yes, we are in jeopardy, but we are better armed than Olasia and Ichthia. Remember, we have merilium."

The monk scratched at his beard. "You have a point, and as I recall, Daneyh's advice to Rhynt was to sail the captured Mystrosian fleet north along the coast of Paudia on their return home. The elves could easily pounce on that fleet or even use a ruse to capture them. Remember, Phendour and Blusk still think the elves are on our side."

"So they capture the ships and then use them to invade Ichthia and then Olasia and then—"

"Enturia," said the Monk. "Come, let's see to those pigeons."

"Aye," said Priss, "but what next?"

"We make it to the cave, pick up Orthor, and head north. If we can get to the coast before the elves, we can hire a fishing boat to take us home."

Priss puffed out a long breath.

"What?" said the monk.

"I was thinking of Zyrx."

The monk blinked. "Oh, no."

43

A small horse covers less ground than a normal-sized horse, particularly when it is towing that normal horse behind it. Zyrx wasn't too worried at first. The sound of the tower building towns as it sped across Paudia had softened and now was barely audible.

He decided to give the horses, not to mention his sore bottom, a rest, pulling up the little horse near the stream he knew would take him to another stream that would lead him to another stream that would take him home.

He sat with his back against a tree and pulled out his pipe. A good pipe helped him think, and it was a distraction from the pain.

It was clear that he and the others had been fooled by Queen Daneyh and her intentions right from the start. And now she had taken an entire country, the largest in the known world, in a single day. What she would do next was the big question. Would she be satisfied with Paudia, or did she want it all?

Zyrx puffed on his pipe and blew out a smoke ring that grew larger and larger and then disappeared just beyond his foot. *Why had she let him go, or the others, when they reached Paudia? It made no sense.*

Zyrx pulled his pipe out of his mouth. "Unless," he said. "Unless, she wants Priss to lead her to Randall's Cave and Orthor." He blinked. "And me to lead them to the Hearth on the Hill."

He tapped the pipe on his shoe, emptying it of its still burning roots, and stomped it out. "Well, we'll just see about that." He stood and climbed on his horse. "Come on, little girl, we have to warn Priss."

He urged the horse forward, then coaxed him to turn northeast. "And if we're lucky, we'll find some friends of mine along the way."

44

Marthe shook his head and grunted. "Stay? Are you truly serious?"

Calax rolled his eyes. Marthe had asked the same questions in different ways at least three times. "Yes, for the last time, yes. There's game. We'll have plenty of food."

"But we'll also have leopards stalking us—and a monster."

Calax rolled his eyes. There is no monster."

"But the body of the king."

"I told you. The leopards could easily come up the staircases to the king's chambers. No, we stay for now, at least until we receive a reply from the queen."

"A bird?"

"Yes."

"But then we go?"

"Depends."

"On the message?"

"Yes, and in the meantime, we can hunt game and see to the repairs on the ships."

Marthe grunted. "Repairs? None needed on my ship."

"True enough, but the other ships were battered by the storm. We will need at least one mast and a keel."

"With the men we have, that is but a day's work, perhaps two. How long will these pigeons take?"

Calax looked into the sky, a habit of his when trying to calculate anything. Math was a fierce warrior to Calax, and full of tricks.

"Um, I'd say a day and a night for the bird we just sent, and the same for the one from the queen."

Marthe nodded, pleased. "Then all the ships will be ready to go. Two more days and we're out of here."

"If," said Calax, "if she says to return to Enturia or continue our voyage. But knowing Queen Rhynt, she may wish to see this for herself."

"By the gods!"

"Patience, Marthe, patience. Use this time to explore the island."

"Explore? I'm no adventurer, Calax. My idea of adventure is eating what my cook serves me."

Calax couldn't help laughing. "I understand that, Marthe, but consider this. There are many myths about Mercadia—if this is Mercadia—and one is of unsurpassable wealth. Gold, jewels—"

"*Gold?* Why didn't you mention that sooner?"

Calax started to answer, but Marthe was already striding away and calling for his mates.

"You, you, and you," cried Marthe. "To me!"

Calax watched them go, then wondered why he wasn't with them. The castle had barely been explored, after all, and there was at least the king's jeweled crown to consider.

Calax called after them. "Hey, wait for me!"

45

Orthor stared at the painted figures on the wall. Six gods standing side by side in a circle, each with a bow over their shoulders and an arrow in their right hands, each arrow a different color: white, blue, green, red, gray, and black. And then, higher up, a young girl in green armor, racing up a hill with three hill tigers, a ravine just in front of them. Do they jump? Is this truly a depiction of Queen Rhynt and Melo, Milo, and Spook?

"Quite a painting."

The voice made Orthor jump, and turn. The Red God was standing behind him. "Do you have to sneak up on a person?"

"Yes, yes I do, particularly when it's a boy withholding information from me."

Orthor tried to stay calm. He'd been thinking about how to react when she next appeared, so he was quick to answer. "Your arrival is propitious."

The Red God cocked her head. "And why is that?"

"I have solved the runes."

The Red God's eyes went wide. "Truly?"

"Yes, I discovered that in addition to the orientation of individual runes and their relation to other runes that—"

"Stop! Just tell me what they say."

Sometimes, the best ruse is the truth. "They describe a land called Mercadia."

The Red God growled at him. "Don't try to fool me. Mercadia is a myth, the stuff of nursery rhymes."

"Myth or no, that's what the runes are all about."

The Red God squinted at him. "You're telling the truth, aren't you? I know when people are lying, and you're not lying."

"Yes, of course I'm telling you the truth."

The Red God frowned, then turned and looked at the painting. "But these figures. Surely there's a story about them in your runes."

"Just pictures."

The Red God shook her head. "No, that can't be." She pointed at the figure with the red arrow. "See here, that's me."

"Looks like a man to me, one of a group of hunters."

The Red God huffed. "I can be a man if I want to. And this is me." Then she pointed at the girl in green armor. "And this has to be Queen Rhynt. Look at that armor, that hair, and those three hill tigers. Who else could it be?"

Orthor went deeper into his planned response. "Are you familiar with *Gander's Book of Nursery Rhymes?*"

The Red God snorted. "I am a god. I don't need books."

"No? Well, there is a story in that book about a little girl who would not obey her parents. Each night, she would secretly leave their house and play in the woods—until she was caught by her father, and punished severely."

"Severely?"

"Yes, her father told her she could not leave the house ever again, and to make his punishment work, he chained the girl to her bed."

"That seems right," said the Red God. "Children should always listen to their parents."

Orthor rolled his eyes, and continued. "The problem for the father, though, was that the chains were not tight enough, so the girl escaped. Now, pay attention, this is where the green armor comes in. To avoid being captured again, she tied leafy branches around herself."

Orthor pointed at the figure of the girl. "See here, you can just make out the shape of a leaf at her waist. She is not wearing armor at all. Just leaves."

The Red God squinted at the figure. "But it looks like armor to me."

"The fault of the artist, I think."

The Red God shook her head. "What about the figures of the gods, then?"

"Again, the artist. According to the story, these figures would be men from the village, sent to look for her when the father discovered her missing again."

"But the figures carry the arrows of the gods."

"What artist doesn't like to spread color around?"

"Then what about the hill tigers? Three of them, not two or four, following Rhynt?"

Orthor sighed. "Back to the story. After a lengthy search, they found the little girl's body, or what was left of it, in a ravine. She had been mauled by hill tigers."

The Red God frowned. "Truly?"

"It's in a book, so . . ."

The Red God started to say something, but then turned as if someone had tapped her on the shoulder. She stood there, silent for a moment, and then turned back to Orthor. "I must go. I am being called."

Orthor shrugged. "Okay, stop in anytime, but I'm done here."

The Red God nodded. "We will meet again." And then she disappeared.

Orthor waited several seconds, then exhaled.

46

The storm had come and gone, leaving Phendour and the rest soaked to the skin and shivering. She peered into the growing darkness, searching ahead for some sign of a building that looked like an inn. But she saw nothing.

She turned to Blusk, who was as miserable as she was. "We must have missed it in the storm."

Blusk looked defeated. "What, we have to retrace our steps? I don't think I can take another step."

"I know, but we can't stay outside much longer. We have to find it."

Blusk looked over at the others, who were trailing behind. "And they seem half dead already."

"Don't say anything to them. We'll walk another few minutes north and then decide what to do."

Blusk nodded. "Then let's move. Standing still does us no good at all."

They walked quietly side by side, crossing what looked like a pasture, and then entering a stand of trees. "We'll cut through here," said Phendour. "With any luck, it will lead us to the inn. This terrain looks familiar to me, and I'm pretty sure we're close."

Blusk nodded and then motioned everyone to follow them into the trees. Two minutes later, they all emerged onto a hill that sloped downward toward a brightly lit town. There must have been twenty buildings, at least.

A town! thought Phendour. *A town? This shouldn't be here.*

Blusk stepped up next to her. "I don't remember any town here, do you?"

"No, just an inn. The rest of the countryside was barren. How could it have changed in so short a time?"

"By the gods!" said Blusk, pointing at the mountains. "Do you see that? Lights, hundreds of lights."

Phendour's mouth dropped open. "What magic is this? Are we really in Paudia. This is . . . impossible."

King Merek and the White Monk walked up beside them, both smiling. "We are saved," said the king. "Hurry, I must get warm, have some food and wine, and tend to my concubines."

"Look," said the White Monk, pointing at the town. "We have a welcoming committee."

Phendour looked back at the town, where a group of men could be seen racing toward them. She smiled at first, but then saw that the men were nocking arrows. She turned back to Blusk and the others. "Run!"

She felt an arrow fly by her ear, then saw it hit in the middle of King Merek's chest, followed by scores of arrows, each hitting its mark. And then something hit her shoulder, hard, again and again. She fell to her knees, then collapsed into the mud. Everything went dark.

Part Five

You seem shocked. Did I not tell you of my intent—my need, my goal, my everything—to exact revenge? Not just on Bookins, but on them all. So now you see the beginning, not that all has gone well. Like you, gods sometimes forget, and I forgot Queen Daneyh—or the wizard or whatever you want to call her or him. The witch had done her work hundreds of years ago, after all, so forgive my forgetfulness. So now she has Paudia in her grip. It is of no matter. I can work with that. Let everyone focus on Paudia as I do my work. To their peril. To their end.

47

Queen Rhynt sat in the council chambers, alternately drumming her fingers on the long council table and glancing over at the fire and her sleeping hill tigers. *Where is Bookins?*

The door answered, swinging open with a loud squeak and a chuckle from Bookins. "Still haven't fixed this door, eh? No matter. Good to have familiar things. Things you can count on, good or not so good."

Queen Rhynt smiled at him. "I'm afraid the theme today is not so good. Come, we have much to discuss." She pointed at a small pile of parchment notes.

"Pigeons, is it?" He picked up his pace and sat down beside her, scooping up one of the parchments.

She immediately put her hand over his. "No, not that one." She grabbed another parchment and handed it to him. "This one first."

Bookins put the other note back into the pile, unrolled the note that she had handed him, and began reading.

Daneyh taking over Paudia by force. Our mission aborted. Fleeing northeast. —Priss

Bookins blinked, and blinked again. "By the gods!"

"Indeed," she said, her anger growing, showing. "I was completely taken in by her. I just can't believe it."

"Don't be so hard on yourself. We should have all known something was wrong when she first appeared. Why didn't she participate in the battle? Why didn't she show herself then?"

"Because she had a plan." Rhynt slammed her hand on the table. "Damn her!"

Bookins grimaced and slumped back in his chair. "And we have trained her warriors."

Rhynt nodded. "Worse, we have shown them how to forge and use merilium. Zyrx will be furious."

"Any word of him in that pile of messages?"

"No, which leads me to believe that he had already parted with the others to return home."

Bookins considered it. "Or they've already taken him."

She put her face in her hands. "Oh, no, it gets even worse."

"What?"

"He had this idea, to build ships out of merilium, to make an invincible fleet for Enturia."

"Wait, wouldn't the ships just sink from the weight?"

She shrugged. "He says no, that they will float, easily."

"Hmph, a curious thing indeed. But do not worry. Zyrx would never build such ships for Daneyh." He paused, then added, "Besides, she doesn't know about his idea."

Rhynt nodded. "I hope that is true, but this queen is very powerful. There is something of the wizard about her."

Bookins sighed, heavily.

"What?"

"You once talked about a wizard who had come out of the tower to help you, and then disappeared."

"Drowned, we think." Her eyes wend wide. "What, you think the queen and the wizard are one and the same?"

"I do not know, but such things have been reported."

"Reported? Where?"

"In scrolls and books. In fact, we have such a book in our library. It's about the early history of Paudia, hundreds and hundreds of years ago, when the land was ruled by elves."

"The same elves, you think?"

"Yes, absolutely."

"So a witch puts them in a tower, where they stay for hundreds of years, until I come along and free them. Oh, great."

"You could not have known."

"Still, I've let loose a power, one we'll certainly have to deal with—if we can."

They both sat in silence for a long minute.

"Wait," said Bookins. "Any word on Orthor?"

"No. He is either fine or taken."

Bookins nodded. "That makes sense. The note said the others were headed northeast. That is the wrong direction if they were going to the caves."

"Why that way?"

"As I recall, there is a fishing village on the northern coast. It would make sense for them to go that way. To get a ship."

"To return home. Good. On the chance that they can't find a ship, I'll send one."

"That's a long voyage, Majesty."

She shook her head. "Not so long. I can send Calax and his fleet to their aide."

"Excellent," said Bookins. He looked down at the little pile of notes. "But what of these other notes?"

Rhynt smiled for the first time. "A miracle of sorts. Calax and his fleet seem to have found the lost world of Mercadia."

Bookins' mouth dropped open.

48

Whelan the Wanderer, Randall Himself, God of All Gods paced back and forth in front of them, his angry demeanor and barely contained silence letting them all know he was anything but pleased.

"I don't know how I came to deserve six gods such as you. My instructions were simple, were they not?" He pointed at the White God. "You, Porto, did you not understand my instructions?"

Porto looked confused. "Of course, and I followed them."

Whelan stopped pacing. "Oh, you did, did you? Please explain, then, why your monk, Phendour, Blusk, and that idiot king of Mystrosia were seen hiking across Paudia."

Porto started to talk, paused, and then began slowly. "Your instructions were to wipe out the fleet. I did that. My storm did that. Yes, a few made it through, but you didn't say I had to kill them all."

"When I say destroy a fleet, I mean totally, ships and men together at the bottom of the sea." He turned on the Green God. "Do you not understand that, Bedo?"

Bedo took a step back, not expecting the sudden assault. "I, I—I do, but you know how unpredictable storms are. Yes, we wind them up, but then it's up to them." He offered a weak smile. "Isn't it?"

Whelan sighed and looked at the heavens in disgust. "You call yourself gods, you prance about like gods, but you have no idea—no idea!—how to actually be gods." He turned back to Bedo. "Tell us, then, of the results of your storm. Are men and ships at the bottom of the sea?"

"No."

"No, of course it's no. They are right now in the harbor of a land I meant to keep safe from the eyes of man."

"Mercadia?" said Bedo. "I thought that was a myth."

"Not hardly."

"And the monster?"

Whelan ignored him and turned on the Red God. "And you, Abo . . ."

"Me what? I have done as you asked. Olasia and Ichthia are as good as in Paudia with their armies fighting each other for control."

Whelan turned to the other gods. "Note how confident she is. She thinks she actually followed my instructions."

"Wait, what?" said Abo. "I did, I definitely did."

"Oh, really. My instructions were for you to create war between Ichthia and Olasia. You sent them to Paudia"

"But the result is the same. They will fight each other."

Whelan rolled his eyes. "But fighting each other means fighting *across* their borders, not outside them."

The Red God crossed her arms and huffed. "Fighting is fighting. Here, there, wherever."

Whelan groaned. "Enough of you." He waved her away. "Now, what about you, Canto? Did you complete your mission? Is Alamaria even now attacking Mystrosia?"

Canto slowly shook his head. "No, but they will. I just need a little more time."

"What, to drink more of their wine?"

Canto smiled. "It is wonderful wine, is it not?"

"Oh, so you thought it a good idea to have your fill of wine before you even started your mission?"

"It seemed a harmless delay, and as I've said—"

"It's wonderful wine. Yes, I know, but don't worry, Canto, you weren't the only god to do nothing. Dado and Indo here also did nothing." He pointed at Dado. "And I would like to know why."

"It was unbelievable," said Dado. "The surprise attack by the elves made it impossible for me to deal with the trolls. Some have been captured, and the rest are scattered over the countryside."

Whelan nodded. "So, in a way, the elves have done your job for you?"

Dado brightened. "Yes, yes, that's true."

Whelan turned to Indo. "And for you as well. The elves have disrupted Paudia better than either of you could do."

Dado and Indo stood silent, heads down.

Whelan shook his head and puffed out a long breath. "It's hard to get good help."

49

Zyrx slowed his horse, pulled him up, and jumped down. There were strange sounds coming from the woods, and he didn't want to ride into a trap. He tied his horse and his packhorse to a Limber Pine and walked slowly to the tree line.

There was a large shape moving through the trees, cutting them down and replacing them with what looked like a small village, the structures plopped down whole, fully assembled, followed by elves who scurried this way and that, making sure the locations were just so.

That damned tower, he thought. *How could I have been fooled so easily? I thought they were my friends.* The sound seemed to be growing louder, so he raced back to the horses and galloped away. He would head east until he could no longer hear the tower at work, and then head northeast again to his goal: the caves.

A mile later, he stopped his horse and listened. Silence. He looked back in the direction he had come from, and sighed. *I might never see the Hearth on the Hill again*, he thought. *Or if I do, it will be surrounded by a damned elf village.*

He shook his head in anger and turned the horses northeast, slowing the pace to a walk. There was no rush now, and he knew a hunter's cabin not far away where he could spend the night and give the horses a good rest.

He wondered what he'd find when he reached the caves. Was Orthor there? Had he solved the runes? What about Priss and the Red Monk? Were they safe? And what the hell were they going to do about Paudia?

He grunted and rode on.

50

As eager as Calax was to receive a return pigeon from the queen, he knew pigeons could only fly so fast, so he kept himself and the crews of the ships as busy as he could. He had split the men into teams, one to take a longboat and chart the island for future voyages, one to scour the island looking for game and anything edible, and one, his and Marthe's team, to explore every nook and cranny of the castle. If there was treasure, Calax felt sure it would be stashed away in the castle somewhere.

Calax had been right about the presence of leopards indicating the presence of game, including big game. By the end of the first day, the food team had found strange, one-eyed rabbits, oxen taller than men, a new species of molfrump, several varieties of squirrels, large flightless birds of many colors, black foxes, and long-tusked pigs. They also found nuts, fruit, mushrooms, and wild berries of every size and color.

When the charting team returned for the day, they brought back clams, mussels, crabs, and large turtles. By the end of the evening's meal, most of the sailors saw no reason to rush away from this island of plenty.

Calax, Marthe, and the rest of his team searched the castle, one floor at a time, starting in the dungeons and working their way up. There was not much to see at first. The lower floors had been stripped clean by the people who had fled. There were a couple of what looked like secret storage places, but those were empty, too. In fact, as they went from cleaned-out floor to cleaned-out floor, Calax and Marthe thought it less likely to find treasure. If the people had indeed fled, they had fled thoroughly.

But when they opened a door on the ground floor, they were astonished to find a vast library filled with dusty scrolls and books, most treatises and observations on Mercadia and its history. Calax's first thought was that Orthor and the Librarian would be as overwhelmed as they would be delighted by the library's contents.

"We will have to send a bird," he said.

Marthe grunted. "Aye, and perhaps there's a scroll or two in here that will tell us more about the monster."

Calax laughed. "Stop with this monster talk. It's a myth, I tell you."

Marthe grunted again. "Maybe."

"Come on, let's call it a day. We'll do the upper floors tomorrow."

"All right, suits me. But there's probably just more nothing up there."

"But perhaps we'll find another room like this one, but filled with gold and jewels."

Marthe rolled his eyes. "More like dust and more dust."

Calax laughed and slapped Marthe on the back. "Well, I guess we'll see, won't we?"

Marthe said nothing, just walked away, leaving Calax at the door to the library.

Calax looked in the library one last time, then closed the door and followed Marthe out of the castle. As they headed back to the harbor, they could see a man running toward them, a pigeon grasped in one hand and a small scroll in the other.

"Here, what's this?" said Calax as the man rushed up, breathless.

"A pige, a pige, a pigeon." The man handed Calax the scroll, then bent over at the waist, gasping for breath.

"What does it say?" said Marthe.

Calax opened the scroll. He was expecting praise for their discovery, but the first word tore away at any notion of that:

Urgent! Elves have taken Paudia. Priss and monk fleeing northeast to fishing village. Make sail at once to rescue them.

"Wow," said Marthe. "I didn't see that coming."

"Nor I," said Calax. "And what village is she talking about?"

"Don't worry, I know the one. It is the only village on the northeastern shore of Paudia."

"What's it called?"

"It's called nothing. Everyone just calls it the village. Handles trade with Olasia and Enturia. I know it well. Been there many times."

Calax nodded. "We'd best get the fleet ready."

"No, not the whole fleet, just the *Marthe*. It's faster than the others. The rest of them will just be a drag on us."

"All right. How fast can we get her ready?"

"A couple of hours. We could be out of here by dusk."

"Then let's get to it."

Marthe turned and began running for the harbor. Calax followed at a slower pace, trying to make sense of the news.

The world seemed upside down.

51

Blusk awoke to the face of an angel staring down at him, and then winced from the pain in his shoulder. "By the gods!"

A girl no older than fifteen, the same age as Queen Rhynt, pushed him back down. "Be still. You'll open your wound."

A familiar voice chimed in. "Do as she says, you big lummox."

"Phendour, is that you?" said Blusk, trying to rise again. The girl pushed him back down. "Be still."

Blusk looked up and focused on her face, which was angelic indeed. "Who are you?"

"They call me Ci, the Seventeenth Concubine of Merek the Mighty, may he rest in his grave."

Blusk remembered now. The volley of arrows, everyone hit and dropping down. "Phendour, are you okay?"

"Yes, a similar wound, meant to stop, not kill. And in case you haven't noticed the jostling, we're in a wagon headed to Port Ochno to see Queen Daneyh."

"Who's that?"

"Ah, a small detail. She and the tower have taken over Paudia."

"But where did she come from?"

"The tower, where she'd been hiding all along."

"I don't understand."

"Remember the wizard?"

"Yes, of course, drowned when the bridge gave way."

"Apparently not. He is the queen, or rather they are one and the same. She has a powerful magic."

"And how do you know all this?"

"One of the guards was one of my best archers. He told me about her, and unfortunately, our plight."

Blusk shook his head. "I don't like the sound of plight."

"No, nor I. We are to be executed in the new public square upon our arrival."

"Oh, wonderful," said Blusk, turning back to the girl. "You said your name is Ci?"

"Yes."

"Is there water?"

"Yes, of course," said Ci. "Let me get it."

She stood from where she had been crouching next to Blusk and moved to the back of the wagon, where a large cistern sat strapped to the wall of the wagon.

She was beautiful, indeed. A little taller than Rhynt, but with long black hair that fell over her shoulders. Her eyes were a green Blusk had never seen before, and twinkled in the light of the lantern swinging above them. She was dressed as all of King Merek's concubines were—in practically nothing. Nothing of her form was hidden by the thin, see-through garment, from her long legs, to her breasts, to her ample behind.

Phendour laughed. "Getting a good look, are you?"

Blusk chuckled. "When it's there to see, I see it."

"Much too young for you, Blusk."

Blusk nodded. "I'll give you that. Could be her father."

"Everyone looks," said Ci, returning with a cup of water. "It doesn't bother me."

Blusk looked her up and down, then smiled. "How is it that you're not injured?"

Ci fought back tears. "My friend Dula. She fell on top of me and took the arrow intended for me. In the aftermath, I tried to run away, but they caught me. I am to be executed along with you."

"Not if I have anything to say about it," said Phendour.

"And me," said Blusk.

Ci wiped her eyes. "Elves are everywhere. I don't see how we can survive."

Blusk grunted. "We've been in worse circumstances, girl. We'll figure it out."

"Aye," said Phendour. "Now, tell us. Are we the only three to survive?"

"I think so. A concubine or two may have been taken, as you might well imagine, but the others are all dead." She shivered. "Very dead. Most took several arrows to the chest, including my king and his monk."

"Both dead?" said Phendour.

She nodded. "Yes, I'm sure of that."

Phendour looked over at Blusk and knew what the next words out of his mouth would be.

"By the gods," he said. "By the gods!"

Zyrx stayed near the main road as much as possible as he made his way toward the caves, but not so close that he could be seen or heard. Occasionally, he could see a patch of the road, but it was always filled with marching elves. He had spent a long time in the Tower, but he had never seen the numbers of elves now dominating Paudia. *Where had they come from? Where were they hiding? Were they really elves or just some fabricated gelas of some kind?*

Zyrx was so lost in his thoughts that he failed to see the river, and almost tumbled in, horses and all. Fortunately, he was able to stop the horses just in time, and backed them away from the rushing water.

He looked downstream and saw what he knew would be there: a bridge. But not *just* a bridge. No, this was the only passable section of the river for miles. If he had missed it, there would have been no way to cross. He would have been forced by the river to end up back in Port Ochno. Not good.

He settled the horses and then approached the bridge with caution. If the elves knew what they were doing, they would have the bridge heavily fortified and guarded, but the closer he got, the clearer it was that the bridge was unguarded.

He urged the horses forward, going from a walk to a trot, the bridge still clear. But as soon as the horses' hooves hit the wood of the bridge, a fearsome troll rushed up from under the bridge and plucked Zyrx off his horse.

Zyrx screamed.

And Bebo laughed. "It me. Bebo. No scream, small one. Just joke. You have joke?"

53

Priss kept them moving at a crisp pace, despite the fact that they had not seen any sign of elves for hours. They were headed northeast, in the direction of a town known by the Red Monk, a fishing village where, if all went well, they would find a boat captain willing to take them back to Enturia.

Queen Rhynt would know by now of their plight, assuming their message got through. If it did, she would no doubt be preparing for war. That's what Priss would do in her shoes. Of course, there was always a chance—a small chance—that she would send a boat for them. Priss knew Calax and his fleet were probably close enough to respond, but in all likelihood, the queen would have summoned Calax home to help with the preparations for war and the defense of Enturia. And Phendour and Blusk would have been too far away to do anything. Her guess was that they had just landed in Mystrosia, returning the king, his monk, and the surviving Mystrosian warriors to their homeland.

The Red Monk broke her from her thoughts, riding up, pointing at the sky. "Look."

Priss scanned the sky. A score or more of seabirds were diving and circling. "We're here?"

"Yes, pull up your horse."

Priss complied, as did everyone behind them. The Red Monk dropped down from his horse and urged the others to do get down. "We camp here for the night. See to your horses. Light a small fire."

Priss was taken aback by his commands. She was the one in charge here, not the Red Monk.

He sensed her displeasure. "Sorry, it's just best to do this quickly. I meant no offense."

Priss nodded. "No offense taken. I see your point." She turned to the other couriers. Some were climbing down, some were still in their saddles. "Do as he says. Now!"

The other couriers dropped down from their horses and began readying the camp.

"If I am not mistaken," said the Red Monk, "we are but a few miles from the coast. Any closer and we wouldn't be able to have a fire, and I know we're all hungry."

"Aye," said Priss. "I'll send a few men on a hunt. We should have rabbits on the spit in no time."

The Red Monk smiled. "That is music to my ears."

"Keep your ears. I would have your eyes right now. What do you far-see?"

He nodded. "Of course." He turned in the direction of the swirling birds and closed his eyes. The images began at once. He could see the coast and the crashing waves. He could see the small village and a few fishing boats arriving and departing. And he could see the tower, dropping down houses and fortifications and hundreds of elf warriors on horseback.

He pulled out of the trance. "By the gods!"

54

Orthor worked his way along the canyon walls, making sure to keep himself and his horses as far away from the river as possible. It was already dusk, the time of the river monster, and he did not want all he had learned about the runes to end up in the stomach of the beast.

Fortunately, he could already see the opening to Randall's Cave just ahead. His horses were tired, but even they realized how close they were, and picked up the pace, going from a walk to a trot without coaxing from Orthor.

Minutes later, having dealt with the horses and tying them in a safe spot close to the opening of the cave, he walked back into Randall's Cave. He had a lot to think about, and a lot to do. He had to recover the scrolls he had left here. He had to write down additional notes about what he had discovered in The Cave of the Six Arrows. And he had to prepare for the journey back to Port Ochno. Without pigeons, he had no choice but to return to Enturia, and a ship from the port was the best and fastest way to get home.

But the first thing he needed was a fire and a cave rat. The fire was the easiest part. He had set a fire before he had left the last time, so all he had to do was pull out his flint and strike it a few times to get the fire going.

As the fire grew, he stalked the dark corners of the cave, looking for rats, his wooden spear held high, ready to thrust at the first opportunity. Twenty thrusts later, he returned to the fire with a typical cave rat: thin and stringy. But it would suffice.

He dressed out the rat and put it on a spit over the fire. It would only take a few minutes, so he plopped down next to the fire and waited.

The fire crackled, the rat sizzled, and Orthor drooled. Then he heard a familiar sound behind him. A pigeon!

He turned and smiled at the bird. He could see right away that it carried a message. "News!"

He stood up and walked over to the bird, coaxing it toward him with a long-practiced warbling whistle. "Come now, I won't hurt you."

"I'm sure you won't," said a voice at the opening to the cave.

Orthor startled and turned to see who it was. An elf in green armor stood there, smiling at him. "Who are you?"

The elf bowed. "I am Slathen, Captain of the First Guard, sent here by the queen to fetch you."

Orthor beamed. "The queen? How wonderful! Let me just get this message off the pigeon . . ."

"No," Slathen said. "Leave the bird. The queen would see you now."

"Now? She's here, in Paudia?"

"Yes, of course."

Orthor couldn't believe it. He had so much to tell her. "Let me gather my things, and we can go."

"No," said Slathen. "Leave everything."

"But I have wonderful things to share with the queen."

He shook his head. "The queen was very specific. She wants you and you alone. Nothing else."

Orthor stood his ground. "I'm not going without my things. Queen Rhynt specifically sent me here to find something, and I have found it."

Slathen laughed. "Queen Rhynt? No, I am talking about Queen Daneyh."

Orthor blinked. "Who?"

55

Calax stood at the stern of the ship, lost in thought, as the island grew smaller and smaller and then disappeared. *Who was this Queen Daneyh and how had she kept herself secret all that time within the tower?* Calax hoped Queen Rhynt and Bookins knew the answers.

But whatever the answers, the world had changed in a moment. The free lands were no longer free, and certainly no destination for sellswords such as himself.

He shook his head. "Here I am once more, thinking of myself first," he said to the breeze, each word blown away to drift above the sea.

He sighed. Priss, the Red Monk, and the team of couriers were in trouble. And he needed to think of them first.

"Why so glum?" said Marthe, coming up behind him. "You look like all is lost, when we have only just begun."

"There is so much to think about."

"Aye, there is that. Paudia, Enturia, our mission, the fate of the lads and lasses we seek to rescue. The world is spinning in every direction you look."

"Yes," said Calax. "And I guess we'd best focus on the task at hand, and let the world unwind on its own."

Marthe laughed. "You really are glum. Take courage in the fact that there is still time—and means—to set things right. She's taken

Paudia, yes, but there's still the rest of the world, and I think our chances are good."

Calax smiled. "Why is it that ship captains are so confident and optimistic?"

Marthe laughed and stretched out his arms. "Look at us. We ride the waved beast every day, never more than a tall wave or a strong wind away from death. Are we optimists? Of course! We have to be to even set foot on this bobbing collection of boards and ropes and sails."

Calax chuckled. "I guess."

"No guess. It's all true. Now, if I may make a suggestion. Turn on your heels and go to the prow of this ship. Look forward, to our rescue mission, and not back to a world that no longer exists."

Calax smiled at him. "Aye, aye, let's do this."

56

Queen Daneyh paced back and forth in front of her thrown. "What word, Clessus?"

Clessus, High Commander of the Armies, an overly tall elf with broad shoulders and a barrel chest, knew to answer quickly. If there was one thing his powerful queen lacked, it was patience. "All is well, Majesty."

"All? Define all, Clessus. And be precise."

"Phendour and Blusk have been taken, and are even now headed here by cart. Also, the young boy, what's his name?"

"Orthor."

"Yes, Orthor. He too has been taken, by Slathen, and should arrive here at the same time as the others, by the same cart."

"Good," said the queen. "And what of Zyrx?"

Clessus frowned. "He has eluded us thus far, but there is no escape now. The entire coast has been taken, and now our forces work back toward the center. It will only be a matter of hours, I think, before we have him as well."

"And what about Priss and the Red Monk?"

"Again, a bit elusive."

"Elusive, elusive. I want found, taken, here."

"Yes, Majesty. "We shall have them soon, I know it."

The queen rolled her eyes. "I hope so . . . for your sake."

A shiver went through Clessus. "Yes, Majesty."

She shook her head and walked over to the throne and sat down. "Now, what news of Ichthia, Olasia, and Alamaria? Have they fallen into our trap?"

Clessus was happy to change the subject. "The forces of Ichthia and Olasia are at sea, both approaching our northern coast."

"Good. Remember to let them advance overland a few miles before taking them."

"Yes, Majesty, the trap is set."

"And what of Alamaria?"

Clessus sighed. "They have been slower to take the bait, Majesty, but they are at least preparing to attack now. And we needn't worry much about them. Their army is small and untrained. I'm sure they'll throw down their arms as soon as they see the size and power of our forces."

"Excellent. And what of our fleets? How many ships have been built thus far?"

Clessus now had good reason to smile. "We are way ahead of schedule. More than 200 ships have been built, floated, and are now at sea. Another 100 ships are being produced every day, and will follow the others to sea in a continuous stream."

"Remember, they are to stay clear of the enemy fleets."

"Yes, Majesty, they will give them wide berth, sneak around them, and attack their homelands."

Queen Daneyh smiled. Everything was going according to plan, except for one thing. "Redouble your efforts to find Zyrx and the missing Enturians. We must have them."

"Yes, Majesty."

"And tell me when they arrive. They will each have an excruciating death, in public."

Clessus nodded. "Yes, Majesty."

She waved him off, and he bowed, turned, and walked out of the throne room. Once outside, he took a deep breath. He had survived another meeting with the queen.

57

Queen Rhynt set down her glass and turned to Bookins, who was tearing into another fried petty hen, which had the advantage of taste without substance. It was said that it took twenty-five petty hens to equal the meat on a single rabbit, and the queen believed it. "They are so small. Why do we bother with them?"

Bookins picked at his teeth with a finger and sucked in the last bit of meat. "The taste, Majesty. It's worth the effort."

"Not for me," she said. "I have no patience with them. Besides, they are such a pretty bird. I'd much rather see them alive and well and not on my plate, fried to nothing."

"I'll have a talk with the kitchen. They expect a queen to want delicacies such as this."

She chuckled. "I'd rather have a simple rabbit stew."

"Indeed. Have no fear, I'll talk to them."

The queen slumped back in her chair and sighed.

"What is it?" said Bookins, leaning forward.

She rolled her eyes. "What is it? It's everything is what it is. And that damned queen—or wizard or whatever *it* is." She pushed back her chair and began pacing back and forth. "What are we to do, Bookins? Paudia is lost, we've had no word from Phendour and Blusk, Priss and the Red Monk are fleeing, and we have no idea what's become of Zyrx and Orthor—they could all be dead by now. And here we sit, near defenseless."

Bookins picked up a napkin, wiped his mouth, and threw it down on the plate. "Defenseless? No, but I see your point. We still have a thousand or so trained troops and all the armor we need to fight, but we are no match for the elves and what they can do with that tower of theirs."

"Then what are we to do?"

Bookins motioned her to sit down. "Sit, sit. I have been thinking of nothing else ever since we learned of Paudia's fall."

She sat down. "So what do you think?"

"First, let's talk about that queen. Her intentions seem clear. She wants to rule all the world, not just Paudia."

"Yes, of course, so she'll be coming for us next."

Bookins shook his head. "No, if she had wanted to do that, she would have taken us first. She was here, the tower was here. It would have been easy."

"Then why didn't she?"

"News of our defeat would get to Olasia and Ichthia, and I think she fears them more than us. She can always come back and take Enturia. There's no rush for us. On the other hand, by taking Paudia, she's put Olasia and Ichthia back on their heels. No, she'll want to deal with them first, I'm sure of it."

"So we have time."

"Yes, but no more than weeks."

She slumped back in her chair. "What good will that do us?"

Bookins laughed. "Time is always good, when you have it. Looking at things from the most positive perspective, we have time for Phendour, Blusk, and the fleet to return; for Calax to rescue the others and return. We'd be much stronger with Calax and especially the fleet. There is much we can do at sea to blunt the attack of the elves."

"But even that may not be enough."

"Indeed, so we need to have allies."

"Allies? Who?"

"If I am not mistaken, Olasia and Ichthia will quickly learn that they cannot face the elves by themselves. They, too, will be looking for allies, as will Alamaria and even the defeated Mystrosians. We should send ambassadors to them all."

"There's no time for that. We're too far away."

"Ah, but the Red Monk is close enough to send gelas."

"As ambassadors?"

"Yes, as ambassadors. If we can get a bird to him or Calax."

Rhynt beamed. "Yes!"

Bookins sighed. "Yes, but my pigeons have never flown that far. The Red Monk is on the move, so it is unlikely that a bird would reach him. And Calax is no doubt at sea again and getting farther and farther away by the minute." He jumped to his feet and started moving toward the door. "Majesty, I'd best see to the birds. I'll send several, including my very best."

"Yes, do that. But return when you're finished. We have much more to discuss."

"Indeed, Majesty, indeed."

58

Priss peered into the distance and squinted. "I do not see what you are seeing."

The Red Monk grunted. "Of course you don't. I am far-seeing, the whole point of which is to see things you can't."

"And you're sure of this?"

"Yes, the elves have taken the port and fortified it. We'll need to skirt it to the right and find a place where we can shelter until Calax and Marthe show up."

Priss frowned. "If they do. I have never used pigeons before. Are they reliable?"

"In my experience, yes they are. Of course, some are more reliable than others and some fall victim to hawks and some just get distracted and fly off."

Priss rolled her eyes. "Thanks for putting me at ease."

The monk chuckled. "Happy to oblige." He looked at the sky and a sliver of a moon rising on the horizon. "Good, it will be quite dark tonight. We go in an hour."

"Why not now, it's dark enough."

"No, I want to send a gela into the town. Explore a bit, check out the ships at anchor. Perhaps there will be a way to get to one."

Priss shook her head. "It sounds hopeless to me. We should go."

He tried not to raise his voice. "*Go*, if you must. I'm staying."

Priss huffed. "No, we'll stay, but make it quick. I don't want to be standing here when the sun rises."

The monk said nothing.

"Did you hear me, old man?"

Nothing.

She took a step closer to him and looked at his eyes, which had grown wide and dark, a sliver of a moon reflecting in them.

59

Orthor stumbled along, his hands tied behind him, as Slathen prodded him with the butt of a spear to move faster. "Move!"

Orthor turned his head to face the elf. "A horse would have helped, you know."

"Quiet!"

"We would have been wherever we're going if we had had horses."

"I said quiet! Or do you want me to gag you again?"

"Very well." Orthor grew quiet and continued on a few steps. "Still . . ."

Slathen tripped him with the spear, and Orthor tumbled to the ground. "We have but a mile to go. Your horses are being tended to, and will follow. Now get up, shut up, and walk or I'll skewer you where you lie."

Orthor managed to get to his knees. "Could I get a hand?"

"No, but you make a fine target there on your knees."

Orthor scrambled to his feet and moved on. "How far?"

Slathen laughed. "A mile, little one, and the faster you get there, the faster you'll have food and drink."

Orthor picked up his pace. "Why didn't you say that before?"

They moved on silently for what Orthor knew was more than a mile until they emerged on a wide dirt road.

"Are we here yet?" said Orthor.

Slathen looked up and down the road. "Yes, now we wait. Sit if you wish."

"You said there would be food."

Slathen motioned him to stop talking. "Listen, little one, do you hear that?"

Orthor heard nothing at first, but then he could just make out the sound of horses, coming closer and closer, their hooves beating out a steady beat. "Horses?"

"Indeed, and food."

Orthor peered down the road, looking for the horses. "Where are they?"

"Patience, they come at their own pace."

And then the horses appeared and the elves riding them, warriors all. "What are you doing here? I don't understand."

Slathen smiled. "The world is changing, little one. Our queen has taken Paudia and soon will take the rest of the known world." He stopped and pointed down the road. "Here it comes."

"It? What it?"

"See for yourself. There, just turning the corner."

"A wagon?"

"Yes, your transportation to Port Ochno and your meeting with the queen."

Orthor watched the wagon's steady progress down the road. Slathen walked down the road to meet it, had a word with the driver, and pointed at Orthor.

The wagon pulled up and stopped beside Orthor. "In the back," said the driver, "and make it quick."

Orthor moved to the back of the wagon, and Slathen climbed up and threw open its curtains. "Up here," he said.

Orthor tried to show Slathen his hands. "And how am I to do that?"

Slathen grunted and jumped down, grabbing Orthor by the waist and lifting him into the darkness of the wagon.

As his eyes adjusted to the light, Orthor could see he was not alone in the wagon. There were three others huddled at the front. A young girl and . . .

"Phendour! Blusk!"

60

It had taken three jokes and a lot of head-scratching on Bebo's part for Zyrx to convince him that the elves were their enemy and that their lives and Enturia were in danger once more. The real clincher was when Zyrx explained to Bebo that Queen Rhynt herself was in danger.

He roared. "No! She good joke teller. Must save, must save."

"Good, good," said Zyrx. "The first thing you need to do is find your armor and your weapons."

"Me have," he said, turning and disappearing under the bridge without another word.

Minutes passed. Long minutes that led to Zyrx pacing back and forth on the bridge, worried that elves would soon be riding over it.

And then Bebo appeared, fully armed, decked out in the amazing merilium armor that Zyrx had made for him.

"Wonderful," said Zyrx. "Now we go. But we must stay off the roads."

"Why?"

"Did you not hear me? The elves."

"No fear elves. Much smaller."

"But there will be a lot of them. More than even a strong troll like yourself could handle."

Bebo snorted. "Pah! Me stronger. Have armor, big sword, shield, spear, and bow with arrows taller than tree."

He had a point, thought Zyrx. *Still.*

"Look, we will go along the road as long as we are not opposed, but if the elves show up, we run."

"Into trees?"

"Yes or just away."

"Away?"

Zyrx sighed. "Bebo, we don't want a fight. We want to get to a village up north where we can book passage to Enturia, maybe even find our friends, too."

"No need boat. Can swim."

Zyrx blinked. He was right. That's how Bebo had traveled to and from Enturia. He was a strong swimmer. "Okay, then let's be on our way. Speed is of the essence."

"Tell joke. Want joke."

Zyrx shook his head. "We must leave, *now.*"

Bebo shook his head even harder. "Joke, *now!*"

Zyrx threw up his arms. "You're impossible, you know that? But what about this. We go, fast, and when we reach the village, I will tell you the joke of all jokes. The best joke ever conceived. The best joke in the world."

Bebo smiled. "Best of best? For true?"

"Yes, for true."

"Me like."

"Good, then, um, let's go."

Bebo was about to reply, but a volley of arrows shot past them, one ricocheting off Bebo's breastplate. Bebo picked up Zyrx, covered him with his shield, and ran.

"Away, Away!"

"Wait," said Zyrx. "My horses!"

But they had already scattered.

"Away, away," shouted Bebo. "Then joke."

61

The Red Monk's gela walked the streets of the rapidly growing village, posing as just another warrior elf. He was asked to do a few tasks by another elf, and did, but for the most part he strolled along in the darkness, taking in everything. If they decided to come through the village, they would have to avoid the central square, which was bustling even at this hour with warriors, as well as builders and their apprentices.

The harbor area was less crowded—a few sailors happy to be ashore. Passing through this area, even boarding a ship, would be less of a problem. Even here, though, there were enough guards to signal a warning. No, they would have to go around the town, find a place where they could signal the *Marthe* unseen.

The Red Monk snapped out of his trance and walked over to the small fire Priss and the others had built. A fine rabbit was sizzling on a spit, eager eyes watching it so intently they didn't notice the monk's approach.

"We have to move, *now*," said the monk, startling everyone.

"By the gods," said Priss, standing. "You nearly scared me to death."

The monk huffed. *Didn't they realize how lucky they were?* "Count yourself lucky. I could have been an elf swinging a sword at your head, and I would have had it and all the other heads around this fire."

"I was just—"

"Entranced, yes, by a little bunny."

"But—"

"Enough of this. The sun will be on us in less than an hour, and we have to make quick time around the village. There is no way through it. And we'll have to be quiet. Walk the horses."

"What about the harbor?" said Priss. "Can we get to it?"

"No, not safe. So douse the fire and let's be on our way. I saw a bluff a mile or so beyond the town. We'll make for that and hope we can signal the *Marthe* from there."

Priss turned to the others. "You heard him. Get moving!"

A whimper came from one of the young couriers. "What about the rabbit?"

Priss walked to the fire and picked up the spit. "Looks done to me. We'll eat it along the way. Now move!"

They doused the fire and began moving east as quickly as they could, but not fast enough to attract the attention of the elves. They worked their way through brambles and a dense wood, climbing with every step. After an hour, the wood gave way to a steep, rock strewn hill.

The Red Monk stopped and looked back toward the village, which was clearly visible from this vantage point. "Come on, faster. The sun is rising, and they will be able to see us clambering up this hill with our horses."

Everyone looked back and nodded silently, too tired to utter words. Their legs were burning from the effort, and the rabbit they had so eagerly gobbled down was no longer providing any help at all.

They huffed and puffed up the hill, tugging the horses behind them and using their hands to pull themselves over the top, where they collapsed just yards away from the edge. The village was behind them now, and the broad sea sparkled below in the rising sun.

They would be safe, for a time.

62

The good ship *Marthe*, with Marthe at the wheel, had sailed through the night in gale winds and high seas. Calax had made it through the night, fighting nausea that came and went with the rise and fall of the waves.

The morning had provided calm seas but little wind, the sails rippling ineffectively instead of billowing and pushing the ship forward at speed. The one good thing is that it gave Marthe and Calax time to recover, though both regretted the slow progress.

Calax met Marthe at the rail of the ship.

"It is a fine sunny day," said Calax.

"Yes, but not a breath of wind," said Marthe.

"What do you think? Will we reach them today?"

Marthe wished he had better news, but in his experience doldrums like this one could last for days. "I am hopeful, but not confident."

"So we're stuck."

"Pretty much."

"Are we on course, at least?"

Marthe looked at the sun. "Pretty much."

"What does that mean?"

"The currents are pushing us a bit far north of east."

"Wait, what, we're drifting backwards?"

Marthe shrugged. "It seems so."

Calax clenched his fist and slammed it on the rail. "Damn!"

Marthe chuckled. "Ha! I had you there. No, we're on course. Just going a bit slow."

Calax growled at him. "You, you . . ." He couldn't help laughing. "You're impossible."

"I know, and ugly to boot."

They fell silent for some minutes, each looking for wind.

"So how far, do you think?"

"If there's no wind, two days. If we get wind, and it's strong, half a day, maybe just six hours or so."

"Well, I guess we're at the mercy of the wind."

"Always." He had another thought. "Say, how far can that monk far-see? Perhaps he knows we're on our way."

"I'm not sure, but I do know one thing. If he can see us, he will send us a sign, perhaps even a gela of himself."

"Good, good. Well, I guess there's nothing to do but wait, for the wind or your monk. You know what I do in such times?"

"No, what?"

"I eat."

Calax laughed. Now that the seas had calmed, his stomach had begun to rumble, in a good way. "Then let's get to it."

63

Queen Rhynt watched Bookins pace back and forth in front of the hearth, the hill tigers following him with their eyes. It was not a pleasant sight. The former fool was old and moved haltingly. His pacing was okay—he did that fairly well, though slowly—but his turns were far from smooth and accompanied by grunts every time he twisted his hips to change direction.

"Enough of the pacing," said the queen. "What shall we do?"

Bookins stopped, rubbed his hip, and moved slowly back to the conference table, where he pulled out a chair and sat down next to her.

"We have sent birds, which should lead to ambassadors, which should lead to allies." He rolled his eyes. "I hope."

"Yes, yes, but what of our defenses? There must be something we can do."

"I have been giving that some thought as well."

"So?"

"First, as to our defenses. We have very little. Twenty fishing boats, ten actual Mystrosian ships, each lightly manned, and six hundred Enturian warriors of varying skill."

"So, pretty much where we were before the Mystrosians attacked."

Bookins shrugged. "Pretty much." He brightened. "Still, we have merilium armor now."

"But the elves have more. More warriors, more weapons, more everything."

"Except ships," said Bookins. "And we'll have an invincible armada once Phendour and Blusk return with the Mystrosian ships."

The queen sighed. "That will be great. On the other hand, the elves have that damned tower. They can build ships, fast, and if they've captured Zyrx, they may have ships made from merilium."

Bookins laughed. "What? Ships made of metal?"

Rhynt frowned. "Don't laugh. Zyrx has a plan for such ships, and if Queen Daneyh catches wind of it, we will be in even more trouble than we are now."

"Seriously? Zyrx really believes . . ."

The queen nodded. "Oh, yeah."

Bookins drummed his fingers on the table. "Then I need to move to the second part of my plan."

"Which is . . ."

He looked her in the eyes, not knowing how she would react, and worried how she would. "Flight."

Rhynt blinked. "Flight?"

He could see anger in her eyes, and disbelief, and a determination to say what he knew she would say. "No!"

Bookins held up his hands. "I know, I know, it is the last thing you want, the last thing *I* want, but if Enturia falls, we need an escape plan."

Rhynt slumped back in her chair. "You are right, but it must be our last option. I will not give up Enturia without a fight."

Bookins nodded, but he knew there were scenarios where flight before fight would be their best option. "Of course, Majesty."

"So what is this plan of your?"

Bookins leaned toward her. "Mercadia, Majesty, *Mercadia.*"

Phendour, Blusk, and Ci sat in front of Orthor, listening intently to his story of runes and gods and Mercadia. Not even the bumpy road and the shouts of the wagon driver to his horses could distract them.

Finally, Orthor grew silent.

"So there really is such a place?" said Phendour. "My mother told me of such a place, but I thought she was making it up. You know, a nursing rhyme with a caution to be good or go to sleep lest the monster get you."

"I'm not sure about the monster," said Orthor. "Your mother may have been right." He turned to Ci, who had been looking at him wide-eyed as he told his story. "Truly, you have nothing to fear from any monster."

Blusk grunted. "I believe every word of your story, including the monster, but the only thing we have to fear now is the elves and that queen of theirs."

"Aye," said Phendour. "We go to our deaths."

"How do you know?" said Orthor. "Perhaps they will return us home."

Ci smirked. "Don't be so silly. Look at your friends and their wounds." She turned to Blusk. "And did they not kill King Merek the Mighty and the White Monk?"

"They did," said Blusk, "and all the others."

"But—" said Orthor.

Phendour raised her hand. "The girl is right. We are on our way to our deaths. We were only spared at first so that our deaths might be more gruesome."

Orthor shook his head. "That can't be true. What have you done? What have I done?"

Ci rolled her eyes. "For a storyteller you are not very wise. Why shoot them in the shoulders if they meant to kill them? And why choose to not kill them when they were wounded and down? Phendour is right, they will kill us all."

Orthor couldn't believe it. "But I have done nothing to them, and neither have you. And we are not wounded."

Ci started to shout at him, but Phendour interrupted. "Perhaps they won't. I can see why they wouldn't harm Ci. She is beautiful and may be of service. As for you, perhaps it's your story they seek."

"Aye," said Blusk, "that's possible, but my coin is on death for all of us, story or beauty or no."

Orthor looked back and forth at them. "Then we must escape."

Blusk's rueful laugh silenced him. "And how do you expect to manage that?"

Orthor took a deep breath. He was tied up. Blusk and Phendour were wounded. The girl, as beautiful as she was, was no threat to the elves. Still, there must be a way. "I read books, and I know things. I will think of a way."

Now everyone laughed.

"You are so silly," said Ci.

He gave her an icy stare. "Perhaps, but I seem to recall a passage in *Whatgig's Guide to Plots, Ploys, Gambits, and Ruses* that just might work."

"Whatzits what?" she said.

"Never mind, I'll think on it." He turned to Phendour. "How much time do you think we have?"

Phendour shrugged. "I have no idea."

"Then I best be quick about it."

"Indeed," said Blusk. "In very deed."

Orthor turned to Ci. "Here, untie me."

65

Priss stood on the edge of the bluff overlooking the sea, looking for any sign of the *Marthe*, but there were only gulls and waves.

They'd spent the night huddled with the horses, without a fire, and now, as the sun rose high, all thoughts were on hot food and a quick rescue.

The Red Monk walked up. "I have far-seen in both directions, to the sea and the town, and all is the same view. Nothing but the sea to the east, and a town busy with construction to the west. The good news, if there is any, is that the elves took no notice of our passing. There will be no search parties looking for us."

"Can we risk a fire?" said Priss.

"No, there is little wood, and besides, the smoke would give us away. No, we'd best keep to dried rat for now."

Priss turned and spit. "Never again. I'd rather starve."

The Red Monk looked around, then bent over and plucked a mushroom from the wet grass. "Well, there are mushrooms."

Priss spit again. "Pah, they're even more disgusting."

The Red Monk laughed. "You have a delicate appetite for a warrior. You must learn to forage, to take what the land and conditions give you." He chomped down on the mushroom and ate it in one bite. "Ah, that is as good as any meat."

Priss rolled her eyes. "Truly?"

The Red Monk looked surprised. "Surely, you have eaten mushrooms."

She shook her head, then nodded. "Once, when I was two, my mother tried to force one on me."

"But the years pass and our tastes change." He reached down and pulled up another mushroom. "Here, take just the merest nibble. If it tastes bad, I'll leave you alone with your strange tastes. If not, then you have enough mushrooms here to fill your gullet."

Priss took it in her hand and sniffed at it. "It smells bad, too." She tried to give it back to him, but he took a step back.

"No, just a nibble. Go on, give it a try."

She took a deep breath and took the smallest bite she could manage, along with a nod of her head. "Hmm, not good, but not awful."

"Again."

She put the remainder of the mushroom in her mouth and chewed with delight. "It is so, so . . ."

"Good?"

"Yes, no—it's *wonderful.* Thank you, d'Abo, for opening my eyes."

The Red Monk laughed. "And your mouth."

Priss started picking up mushrooms one after the other and stuffing them into her mouth. "Bi-di-gids."

"What?"

She finished chewing. "I said, *by the gods!*"

The Red Monk's laugh was short-lived. Something was on the horizon. "Wait, what's this?"

Priss turned and looked out to sea. "What? I see nothing."

The Red Monk was already in a trance, far-seeing.

"What is it?"

He dropped out of his trance. "Ships, scores of ships, perhaps a hundred or more."

"Could it be Calax and his fleet?"

"No, he did not have that many ships."

"Then who?"

The Red Monk puffed out a big breath. "Olasians."

66

"Olasians?" said Queen Daneyh, rising from her throne. "Are you sure?"

Clessus thought to take a step back as she approached, but he decided to stand his ground. *She is angry at the news*, he thought, *not me. I hope.* "Yes, Majesty, more than a hundred ships, each flying King Wazapor's bull sigil."

Her laugh surprised him. It sounded more like a cackle. "We have them, we have them!"

"Majesty?"

"Don't you see, Clessus? They have fallen into the trap."

"But Majesty, we are not yet at strength at the northern port. The tower has much left to do. They will sweep over us like we weren't even there."

She nodded and waggled her eyebrows. "Exactly, exactly. They will think their task easy and drive deeper into Paudia." She smiled. "And then we'll destroy them."

"But Majesty, there are hundreds of women and children there. The loss of life will be huge."

She waved him off. "Worth the loss."

Clessus blinked. "Majesty, surely . . ."

She thrust her finger at him. "Clessus, you know what's wrong with you? You're *weak*. War brings death. It is part of the grim dance."

"Majesty, at least get them into the tower."

She rolled her eyes. "If we do that now, it will seem planned, part of a ruse. The Olasians will be cautious when I want them to be headlong. No, no one is to go into the tower until the Olasians actually come ashore."

"But—"

"But once they attack, then and only then may the tower take in the women and children."

He thought to speak but she raised her hand. "Enough. I have spoken. Make sure my orders are carried out explicitly."

Clessus nodded.

"And if those orders go awry, it will be your head."

The wind came out of the east, light and breezy at first, then growing stronger, billowing the sails and lifting the *Marthe* in the water and pushing her west, faster and faster. The Olasian fleet, once just specks on the horizon, was growing larger by the minute.

Calax joined Marthe at the wheel and pointed at the fleet. "We will be seen."

Marthe shrugged. "Sooner or later, yes, but the *Marthe* is no warship. More a converted fishing boat."

"Still."

"Why so nervous? We are nothing more than a trade ship, one the Olasians had seen many times in my travels. And I doubt those who know me have forgotten my misshapen face."

Calax shook his head. "Still."

Marthe huffed. "Oh, all right, I'll take her closer to the coastline. Then they will definitely think me nothing more than a fishing boat returning to port."

Calax seemed relieved. "Good, good."

Marthe spun the wheel and the ship began moving south toward the coast of Paudia. "Satisfied?"

Calax smiled. "Yes."

Marthe glanced over his shoulder at the Olasian fleet. "Well, you shouldn't be." He pointed at the fleet. A group of six warships had separated from the main group, and were now approaching them at full sail.

"By the gods!" screamed Calax.

Marthe laughed. "You and your gods. Have you forgotten that the *Marthe* is the fastest boat in the world?"

"But there are half a dozen of them."

"We will lose them all, but I will have to turn east to make them understand they can't catch us."

"But the rescue?"

Marthe grunted. "First we rescue *us*, then we rescue them." He spun the wheel and the boat groaned east.

68

Bebo ran with Zyrx in his arms for over an hour, finally stopping at the edge of a deep wood.

He dropped Zyrx to the ground, then bent over and gasped for breath. "Big run. Small air."

Zyrx was happy to be on the ground again, though his legs were asleep from the strength of Bebo's grip on them. He sunk to the ground and rubbed at his legs until they came back to life, then laughed. "Did we have to run so far?"

"Run means run. I do quick."

"You do, you do."

Bebo turned to the wood. "We go in. Dark good."

Zyrx peered into the wood. Bebo was right. He could barely see into it more than ten feet, then it was just black. "Are you sure?"

"Me do many times. No worries. Come."

Zyrx stood and followed Bebo into the wood. "Wait for me."

"Stay close. No lose."

Zyrx grabbed onto the bottom of Bebo's trousers and tried to keep up. "Slow down."

Bebo slowed his pace, but only slightly. "Still need go quick." He reached down and lifted Zyrx into his arms once more, and then began to run headlong into the darkness.

A few minutes later, he suddenly stopped.

"What?" said Zyrx.

"Listen."

Zyrx heard nothing. "But—"

"Quiet. Horses. Wagon."

Bebo made his way toward the tree line, the darkness falling away, revealing a road filled with elf warriors escorting a small wagon.

As the wagon passed, Zyrx caught sight of Orthor sitting in the back of the wagon. "Oh, no."

"What?"

"A friend of mine, taken by the elves."

"Where friend?"

"There, in the back of the wagon. We need to find a way to rescue him."

Bebo charged out of the wood without saying a word, Zyrx hanging on for dear life. He knocked the driver out of the wagon, sat Zyrx in the driver's seat, and roared, "Go!"

Zyrx grabbed the reins and coaxed the terrified horses forward, running over startled elves as they went. Bebo brought up the rear, swinging his sword as he ran, elves dropping left and right, his shield held high to block the arrows that eventually came, but were too late and too few to cause harm.

A mile down the road, Bebo ran to the front of the wagon and told Zyrx to pull up. Zyrx pulled hard on the reins, but the horses were so terrified, it took him several minutes to get them to stop.

Once stopped, Zyrx dropped the reins and looked back into the wagon, his eyes going wide. "Phendour? Blusk?"

"And me," said Orthor.

"And me," said Ci.

Zyrx laughed. "By the gods!"

"Well, at least one god," said a voice behind him.

He turned to see a beautiful red-headed woman standing next to the wagon. "Who are you?"

"I am known by many names, but Orthor there knows me as Abo, the Red God." She cocked her head. "And he owes me."

69

Priss and the Red Monk stood on the very edge of the bluff, not believing what they were seeing.

"They're running away!" said Priss.

"As they should," said d'Abo. "But look closely, Marthe is putting distance between the *Marthe* and those warships. Those ships will break away from the hunt soon enough."

"But will they be back?"

The Red Monk raised his eyebrows. "Of course they will."

Priss sighed. The *Marthe* was even farther away now. "I guess."

"No guessing, lass. They will sneak back tonight in the cover of darkness. We need to be ready."

"What, a whole day without a fire?"

The Red Monk held up a finger. "Wait, let me see what's happening in the town?" He fell into a trance and just as quickly broke away from it. "Ha! The town is in disarray, elves running everywhere. They've seen the ships."

"So?"

"So we can have a fire, even a bonfire, without attracting their attention." He turned in a circle, his eyes closed. "Yes, there's molfrumps a hundred yards that way. I count six, no seven, and they're as plump as tongos."

Priss followed his finger. "I see them!" She pulled her bow from her back and an arrow from her quiver. "See to the fire, I'll be back with all seven."

The Red Monk watched her run away. *Oh, to be young again and run like that*, he thought. Then he turned and looked out to sea. The Olasian ships had broken away from the hunt and were returning to their fleet. The *Marthe* was out of sight, somewhere to the east.

He heard Priss shout in the distance. It was a joyful shout, a yip. *Well, we at least have one molfrump. I'd best see to the fire.*

70

Orthor and the Red God sat across from one other in the wagon, locked in a staring contest. Orthor was wavering—he had no idea how long he could stare down a god. The god, on the other hand, could stare all day, and smiled at him to suggest his folly.

Finally, she rolled her eyes, and laughed. "Orthor, Orthor, Orthor. You cannot remain silent in the face of a god. Have you forgotten your promise—to let me know first what you found in the caves?"

Orthor took a deep breath. *What can I tell her that would not betray my promise to the queen?* "I have told you all I know. The runes in Randall's Cave tell the history of Mercadia and its destruction by a volcano. If you want to know more than that, you'll have to retrieve the scrolls I wrote, which are hidden in the cave."

She squinted at him. "Are you telling me everything? Are the runes not known as the *Word,* the basis for everything?"

Orthor shrugged. "Only if Mercadia itself is the Word."

She shook her head. "And what of the cave paintings in The Cave of the Six Arrows, all the gods gathered together watching a girl and her tigers run toward a cliff?"

"Who knows? Just paintings as far as I could determine. An obscure legend, perhaps, as I have told you."

"And did you not find it curious that your queen looks like that girl and also has three hill tigers?"

"Yes, of course, but it could still be a coincidence. In my time with her, she never mentioned meeting all the gods. Certainly that would have been something I would have told everyone. Wouldn't you?"

She grunted. "I *am* a god, and I see the others almost *every* day."

"Then why not ask them. And why do you want to know about all of this? It makes no sense to me."

The Red God looked like she had been slapped. "Of course it doesn't, but I will tell you this. The gods, or at least some of us, are not happy. We do not like what is happening to the world, and we would change it, if we could. The runes may have an answer; that is why."

Orthor shrugged. "Well, I keep telling you, that's all I know. If you want to know more, you'll need to retrieve the scrolls and have me explain them to you."

She turned away from him and shouted at Zyrx, who was driving the wagon. "When you reach the tall pines, turn left. That will take you to the northern port, where you should be able to find passage back to Enturia."

And with that, she disappeared.

71

Marthe and his crew cheered when they saw the Olasian ships end their pursuit and break away, heading back to their fleet.

"How's *that*, Calax," he shouted.

Calax smiled, then clapped his hands. "Amazing, and very welcome."

Marthe waggled his eyebrows. "And now comes the fun. We'll sail east for half an hour and then strike our sails and set anchor. Then, at dusk, we'll set sail again, heading west along the coast, keeping close in until we can see the port and assess the situation."

Calax nodded. "We'll have to keep an eye out for Priss, the monk, and the couriers."

"Of course, but we don't want to fall into a trap, either."

Calax frowned.

"What? Why the frown?"

"The Olasians. I would have never predicted that they would attack Paudia."

"They come to fight the elves, do they not? That's a good thing, isn't it?"

"I don't know. King Wazapor is a cautious man. I've fought both for him and against him, and this move is totally unlike him. No, someone has gotten in his ear, shown him some advantage to be gained, and gained easily."

"I see what you mean. And he's left Olasia open for attack by the Ichthians."

"Yes, he has, which is even more unlike him. He hates Ichthia to his very bones. This risk he is taking must have an incalculable reward for him. Otherwise, it makes no sense."

"And the more I think of it, what of the Ichthians?"

"What do you mean?"

"I mean what if the Ichthians are also attacking, and they know that the Olasians are attacking, and both know that each other is attacking?"

"You mean they're now allies?"

"Yes, in a word."

Calax shook his head. "No, I don't see it. If the Ichthians are attacking, they're acting independently. I'm sure of it."

"So . . ."

"So we need to get to the Red Monk and the others sooner rather than later. Queen Rhynt needs to know this."

"We could send a bird."

"Yes, we will, but the Red Monk has powers we and she can use." He pointed west. "To the port, now, at full sail!"

72

Priss sat on the edge of the bluff with the rest of them, watching the approach of the Olasian fleet. Some tried to count the number of ships but lost count; there were just too many of them. When Priss looked left, she could see the entire port and part of the village and fortifications that the elves had built. There didn't seem to be much movement of their warriors, or any sense of alarm at all.

"Why aren't they responding?" she said.

"I don't know," said d'Abo. "Perhaps they are laying a trap of some sort."

"Drawing them in?"

"Yes."

"No, that would only make sense if the elves had their own fleet. As far as I know, they have no ships."

"Good thinking, but perhaps the elves' plan is to draw them deeper into Paudia and then attack them on land."

Priss nodded. "You're probably right, but it seems a big risk to give your enemy a foothold on your land."

The Red Monk grunted, but said nothing.

"So," said Priss, "when do you think they'll come back for us?"

The monk looked east along the coast. "If I were them, I'd find safe harbor not far away, and then return at dawn, keeping close to the coast."

"Can you far-see to check that out?"

The monk blinked. *Of course I could.* "Yes, give me a moment."

He dropped into a trance and looked as far as he could see down the coast. A white dot appeared and began to grow in size by the second. He dropped out of the trance. "They're coming! At full sail!"

Priss leaped to her feet. "Where?"

"From the west, along the coast. It's the *Marthe!*"

Priss turned to tell everyone to prepare to leave, and froze.

A troll was peering over the edge of the same embankment they had climbed to reach the bluff.

She drew her sword, then dropped it to her side. "Bebo?"

Part Six

I'm sorry. I have to pause here a moment. Everything was going so well—the Mystrosian fleet destroyed, the elves firmly in control of Paudia, all chaos about to unfold from the almost simultaneous attacks of the Ichthians and the Olasians, and Enturia and Queen Rhynt near defenseless—but now I must tell you something that strikes at my heart. No, not the fact that several Enturians had at this point escaped my wrath. No, sometimes details go astray in the maelstrom. I know that. You know that. No, what strikes at my heart is disloyalty. Abject disloyalty, and the very worst kind. Disloyalty by a god. My god. So forgive me if I seem to be telling what must be told through gritted teeth, for my anger, even in those days, was beyond imagination.

73

The fire in the hearth had reduced itself to nothing more than glowing embers as Queen Rhynt, Bookins, and Whelan continued their talks about what should be done next. There was no agreement. The queen wanted to attack Paudia, particularly after the message from the latest bird. The Olasians and perhaps the Ichthians were attacking. Why not join them in the fight?

Bookins had counseled against that, arguing that they did not have the strength or resources to launch a successful campaign, even with the aid of other countries. Instead, he suggested that they fortify the city as much as they could, but have in place an escape plan. Ships stationed along the north coast, perhaps.

Whelan shook his head at both plans. He thought they should flee to Alamaria, arguing that it had always been neutral in most conflicts. And besides, it had the best wines.

Queen Rhynt had rolled her eyes at that. "You always think of your own pleasure first, don't you?"

"Majesty, pleasure is an important consideration."

"Not now it isn't. Right now our only concerns are survival and putting an end to Queen Daneyh."

Bookins interrupted. "The queen is right, and besides, Alamaria is too far away."

Whelan slumped back in his chair. "Well, what about Didu or even Mystrosia—we defeated them, after all. Why not seize their lands?"

"No, I'm not that kind of queen."

Whelan laughed. "Majesty, I applauded your actions after our victory, but now we are in a different world. Largesse is something we cannot afford. We defeated them fair and square and—"

Rhynt and Bookins shouted at the same time. "No!"

Their shouts woke up the hill tigers, if only briefly, just long enough for them to turn in circles and plop back down in front of the hearth again.

"There is another option," said Bookins. "Wait for Calax and the others to return. They've seen the Olasians' attack, and Priss and the Red Monk have seen the fortifications of the elves. They have valuable information, information that could guide us to the best path forward."

The queen nodded, then drummed her fingers on the table. "Yes, and no."

Bookins blinked. "What?"

"Time is of the essence, whatever our plan. So let's meet them halfway, at that island they discovered."

Bookins started to object, then closed his mouth, offering nothing more than, "Hmm."

And Whelan groaned. "An unknown island, somewhere in the Great Sea? You can't be serious."

"Oh, but I am," said Rhynt. "An island known only to us. Plus, we'll all be together again." She stood and leaned across the table at Bookins. "Send a bird to them and make ready our ships, we leave on the tide."

74

Calax watched Bebo swimming effortlessly alongside the *Marthe.* "How does he do it? You would think his very mass would sink him at once."

Marthe shrugged. "I don't know, but we surely couldn't take him aboard without endangering the ship and all aboard. He'd sink us sure."

"Aye." Calax looked around the crowded deck. Phendour and Blusk sat near the door to the captain's cabin, being tended by Ci. Their wounds were healing nicely thanks to her.

Orthor, the strange boy Rhynt had sent to the caves to discover—what? He didn't know. Something about that picture of her and her hill tigers. Or maybe someone else. He stood on the rail, looking green and queasy.

Priss and the many couriers stood aft, tending to the horses. Zyrx and the Red Monk were in animated conversation, an argument of some kind. Calax would have to find out about what.

"You seem lost in thought," said Marthe.

"What? Oh, yes. Just wondering what the next days will bring."

"The queen's bird?"

"Aye, I don't like her decision. Abandoning Enturia."

"We don't know that. She just said she was coming."

"Maybe, but knowing her, she will bring every able-bodied man and woman with her."

"But knowing Bookins, I doubt he would let her. No, they will bring a strong force, but not everyone. They will leave behind enough men to at least create the illusion that Enturia is ready for anything."

"I hope you are right, but Rhynt is strong-willed and stubborn. And now that she's queen, well . . . who knows what she'll do?"

A strong gust of wind nearly took them both off their feet. "Well now, what's this?" said Marthe. He looked at the sky and then the waves. "Something's brewing. I'd best see to the sails."

75

The tide came and went, and came and went again until two ships left the port for Mercadia, if indeed the island discovered by Calax was really the home of that lost civilization.

Former King Braque, now Lord Braque, stood on the docks with the more than five hundred warriors selected to defend Enturia in Queen Rhynt's absence, or at least give the appearance of a defense. They would line the battlements, giving any attacker the impression that they were at full strength.

She had bestowed upon him the temporary title of regent, which seemed to please him. He was still struggling with his embarrassment at the Battle of the Plain of Sorrows, and hoped to make up for it by defending the land he ruled for many years.

Bookins, despite his years, had decided to go with Queen Rhynt, to offer her council in whatever way he could. He was also excited to see this new island. He had read books about Mercadia, and it would be interesting to see how well the second-hand accounts and myths held up to the real thing.

He and Rhynt and Whelan had stood on the rail, waving at the men on the docks until the docks were too small to see.

"I wonder if we will ever see Enturia again," said Rhynt.

"Well, I'm sure *you* will," said Bookins. "As for me, at my age, it's not wise to make predictions about anything, including your next meal."

Whelan laughed. "You say it true, my friend. But we will at least have an adventure, maybe write some songs to be sung down through the ages, and isn't that what life is all about?"

Bookins shrugged. "For you, maybe. I find that adventure makes me jittery and sours my stomach. The unknown, you see, when all I want is extended monotony, the familiar."

"And yet you came," said Rhynt. "Why?"

"Well, they say a *little* adventure never hurt anyone, so . . ."

So they sailed on.

76

The Red Monk stood at the prow of the *Marthe*, in a deep trance. He wanted to see what lay ahead, particularly this new island Calax had spoken about. His far-vision had taken him across the waves to see gulls and breaching whales—and an island seemingly in flames.

He broke from his trance and raced back to the wheel of the ship, where Marthe stood with Calax. "There's something wrong."

Calax blinked. "Wrong?"

"Your island, it seems to be on fire."

Calax's eyes went wide. "Fire? What exactly did you see?"

The Red Monk pointed west. "A great fire on the southern end of the island. There, see the smoke?"

Calax walked to the prow. A billowing column of smoke was rising from the horizon. He yelled back to Marthe. "Can we make the ship go faster?"

Marthe looked up at the sails. "Yes, we can add another sail, but it's a small sail and won't increase our speed that much."

"Do it, we need to get there as fast as we can." He looked at the horizon again. The shape of an island began to appear under the smoke. He could see a great orange spot, the fire itself, on the southern end of the island, just as the Red Monk had said. "The island's not on fire—it's our ships!"

The Red Monk dropped back into his trance long enough to confirm what Calax had said. "Yes, in the harbor. All are ablaze."

"My fleet!" Calax shouted.

His shout drew everyone on deck, and Orthor was the first to utter the question on everyone's mind. "What now?"

77

Whelan was the first to see the smoke, and smiled slyly when he saw it. *The plan unfolds*, he thought.

He waited a few minutes, hoping that someone else would notice it, but the sailors were busy with sails and ropes and Rhynt and Bookins were deep in conversation, each raising their fingers into the air to make their points.

Finally, he had had enough. "Smoke!"

Everyone stopped what they were doing and looked at Whelan, who pointed at the horizon. "There!"

Rhynt and Bookins walked up to him.

"What do you make of it?" said Rhynt.

"A fire," said Whelan. "On the island."

"But which island?" said Bookins.

Whelan looked at Bookins like he was crazy. "*The* island."

Bookins turned to Rhynt. "Is that the right direction for Calax's island?"

Rhynt looked at the position of the sun. "Yes, it can only be his island."

"Do you think it's a signal fire?" said Bookins. "You know, to guide us?"

Whelan laughed. "Bookins, you act the fool once more. Anyone can see that fire is too large to be a signal fire."

Rhynt looked around the deck. "Where's the captain?"

"In his cabin, I suspect," said Bookins. "Doing captain things."

"Whelan," she said, "would you be so kind as to fetch that man and see if he can get more speed out of this ship?"

"With pleasure, Majesty." He bowed with a flourish and strode away, whistling.

Bookins watched him go. "Why is he so happy?"

Rhynt shrugged. "Perhaps he feels a new song coming on."

She began pacing, then stopped. "Bookins, see if you can find a signalman. We need to let the other ship know that we will be adding sails and making for the island as fast as we can."

He wasn't even sure what a signalman looked like, but he nodded and walked away toward a group of sailors. Perhaps they would know.

78

Calax stood at the prow of the *Marthe,* his face ashen, staring at the burned out hulks of the ships in the harbor. "How could this happen?"

"Lightning, perhaps?" said the Red Monk.

"But there was no storm."

"Some storms contain but a single bolt. That bolt could have struck one ship and started the fire that spread to the others."

"But where are the men? They can't all have been trapped below."

The Red Monk nodded. "Let me see what I can see."

He dropped into a trance and looked inside the ships. There was not a single person or a single body. He looked at the castle and roamed its rooms and halls. Not a single person or body. He walked through the jungle for as far as he could see, and again nothing.

He broke from his trance. "There is no one onboard the ships, in the castle, or as far as a mile into the jungle."

"But they could have fled to the far end of the island, right?"

The Red Monk shook his head. No, Calax, no."

"What do you mean? Of course they could."

"No, Calax, I saw no person or bodies, that's true, but what I did see was blood—*everywhere.*"

79

Rhynt dropped out of her trance, and gasped. "The ships—*the ships!*—are on fire."

Bookins, at her side along the ship's rail, squinted at the horizon, and saw nothing. "What? What ships? Whose ships?"

She fought back tears. "Ours. Calax and his fleet. In flames."

Bookins didn't know what to say. *Could it be true?* "Majesty, no, no, no."

She clenched her fists. "Who could have done this? Who!"

Bookins took a step back. He had never seen her so quick to anger. "Majesty, wait, slow down. Tell me exactly what you saw."

She began pacing up and down. "Ships. In a harbor. Next to an island. The island we seek. All in flames."

Bookins looked at the position of the sun. "Majesty, not even the *Marthe* is fast enough to travel so far, so quickly."

She blinked. "What?"

"Calax. He is still at sea. He must be."

She looked at the horizon. "Truly?"

"Yes, Majesty. Whatever happened to the other ships has not happened to the *Marthe*."

She nodded, then wiped away her tears. "We must get there at once."

"Yes, you must," said a voice behind them. They turned to see a wavering image of the Red Monk, who was hovering a foot off the deck. "It is as Bookins says. We are fine, but the rest of the fleet—and its men—are gone."

Rhynt breathed a heavy sigh. "But how?"

"We do not yet know. I will tell you all there is to know when you arrive. We have anchored just outside the harbor and will await your arrival before proceeding to the island itself."

And with that, the image faded away.

80

Queen Daneyh squinted at the messenger, who was standing in front of her, shaking.

"Say that again," she said.

The young elf, who was barely past his first chin shaving, stammered the words again.

Daneyh waved him away. "Go, and never let me see your face again."

The young elf attempted a bow, failed, and then fled the throne room.

She turned to Clessus. "You heard that?"

"Yes, Majesty."

"And what would you recommend we do?"

Clessus hated these situations where she asked his opinion. He knew his opinion didn't matter—at all. She had made up her mind. His job was to guess what she had decided. And now, judging from the way she was looking at him, there could be little doubt that she wanted the prisoners back, at any cost. It was a power thing, a control thing. "Majesty, we must go after them."

She cocked her head. "You know me well, Clessus. Yes, do whatever you need to do to bring them back. I want to see them in chains, in this room, on their knees."

"Yes, Majesty."

"And don't spare any resource. Take ships, horses, warriors, whatever you need."

Clessus blinked. Did she really mean he was to lead this effort? "Majesty, to be clear, you want me to handle this mission personally?"

She looked him up and down. "Who better to lead?"

Clessus bowed. "Yes, Majesty, I will see to it."

"And make sure you're quick about it."

"Majesty, they are already at sea. It will take days, perhaps weeks to track them down."

Daneyh rolled her eyes. "Track them down? You know very well where they're going—Enturia. If you leave on the tide, I'm sure you can intercept them even before they reach home."

"Yes, Majesty." He bowed, turned, and strode out of the room, taking in a deep breath as soon as he was out of her view.

This could mean my head, he thought. And that thought had him running for the docks.

81

Bookins spotted the *Marthe* first. "There!"

Rhynt squinted, but couldn't see it. She dropped into a trance, and smiled. "Yes, I can see the burnt-out ships and the *Marthe* at anchor." She dropped out of her trance. "All is well, or seems to be."

"Good, good."

"I reckon we will arrive in an hour."

Bookins looked at the dot on the horizon. "Do you think? It looks farther away than that."

"No, when I far-see, I pretty much become aware of the distance."

Bookins smiled. "Well, of course you do."

"Now, the first thing I want to do when we arrive is take the longboat to the *Marthe*. They have much to tell us."

"Yes, Majesty, I'll see to its readiness at once." He bowed and walked away.

Rhynt looked at the growing dot on the horizon, and dropped into a trance again. She could see everyone on deck, looking back toward her fleet. They were all smiling. Calax and Marthe were in deep conversation. A young girl was tending to the wounds of Phendour and Blusk. Zyrx sat nearby, eating an apple with a small knife, not far away from Orthor, who did the same.

And then a large mass blocked her vision. She blinked a few times, and it came into focus: Bebo!

She dropped out of her trance, and laughed. "Oh, my, looks like I'll need more than a few jokes."

82

Whelan, Randall Himself, God of Gods, looked at Canto, the Blue God, and Canto looked away.

"You had one job," he said. "One. But is Alamaria striking or even preparing to strike Paudia?"

"No."

"And why is that?"

"They have no interest in or capacity for war. They are vintners, and mostly drunk."

"Perhaps we should spoil their harvest."

Canto looked alarmed. "But then we wouldn't have wine."

The god had a point. "Then perhaps I can assign another job to you."

Canto cringed. "Yes, um, of course."

"Good, good. We will leave Alamaria to its drinking, at least for a time. Instead, I'd like you to go to Mystrosia. They are without a king or even a monk. Create chaos, faction against faction, until we have a new king, one we can easily manipulate."

"But I know nothing of Mystrosia."

Whelan turned on him, his voice rising with each word. "You will learn."

"Yes, yes, of course."

Whelan turned away from him and pointed at Dado, the Gray God. "And you, how is it that one of the trolls escaped Paudia and is even now helping Calax and Queen Rhynt?"

The Gray God looked confused. "I, I—what?"

"Bebo, the one who helped Bookins with his gambit against us."

Dado shook his head. "I don't know. I thought he was rounded up with the others."

Whelan shook his head. "Well, I can at least give you some credit for that."

Dado smiled.

"But it's nothing to smile about."

"No, of course not."

Whelan turned to point at Abo, the Red God. "And you, Abo . . ."

But there was no Abo.

"Where is she?"

The other gods shrugged.

"Insolence!"

83

Queen Rhynt's fleet arrived at dusk, when the island was already shrouded in darkness. She could make out the harbor and the smoldering ships and the silhouette of what appeared to be a grand castle hard upon a vast jungle, but all detail was lost.

She ordered the longboat lowered, and she and Bookins and a few oarsmen climbed aboard and, with the help of lanterns and shouts, made their way to the *Marthe*. Rhynt was the first to clamber out of the boat and onto the deck, where she jumped into the arms of Calax. He took her in his arms and gave her a big hug, and then lowered her to the deck once more.

"Majesty, it is so wonderful to see you."

"And you," she said, then noticed the others walking toward her, all smiles and open arms. She gave Zyrx and Orthor big hugs, then turned to Phendour and Blusk, giving each light hugs recognizing their injuries. Priss squeezed her so hard, she lost her breath, only regaining it in time to receive an equally strong hug from a man she once hated: d'Abo, the Red Monk.

And then came Ci. Rhynt wasn't sure what to make of the beautiful little girl, who was not much younger than she was.

"They call me Ci, Majesty," she said, stepping forward. "A concubine in the service of my late king."

Rhynt's eyes went wide. "Late?"

"Yes," said Phendour. "Taken down along with his monk the same time we received our injuries."

"Oh, my," said Rhynt, then looked at Ci. "You are welcome among us, and will serve, but not as a concubine. More a lady in my court, or whatever your heart desires."

Ci curtsied. "Thank you, Majesty."

Rhynt looked around. "Where's Bebo? I have a special joke for him."

"Swimming around the island, to see if he can find any reason for the slaughter that has happened here."

Rhynt looked at the island, which was now in total darkness. "I would hear everything, now."

Calax nodded. "I thought as much. Marthe's cook has prepared a grand meal for us."

"How wonderful!"

Calax motioned her toward the captain's cabin. "Come, Majesty, the meal is ready."

She followed him down the deck, and then suddenly stopped.

"What is it, Majesty?"

"Whelan. I thought he was with us."

Calax rolled his eyes. "That man has a way of disappearing. My guess is that he's still on your ship."

She shrugged. "I guess." "Well, more food for us, then," said Calax.

"Indeed," she said with a smile.

She turned and looked at the island, and wondered whether she was ready for what might come in the morning.

84

Lord Braque paced back and forth along the parapet. Everything was ready, at least from his perspective. He had spread his forces along the fortifications facing west toward Paudia. If an attack was coming, it would come from that direction. The elves knew about the dangers on the east of Enturia—sucking mud and all manner of beasts—so they would not make the mistake the Mystrosians made. He had also taken advantage of one of Bookins' ploys—placing their fastest fishing vessel far out to sea as a spotter to provide early warning.

He had thought briefly about using another of Bookins' ploys—tempting the elves into the harbor where they could be trapped and dealt with swiftly—but he knew the elves wouldn't take the bait.

He also knew that their chances against any sizable force were dismal. They might be able to hold the castle for a few days, perhaps a week, but any protracted battle would find them on the losing end.

With such prospects, he thought it wise to have pigeons ready, one with a message of victory, another for defeat, and several others for come what may.

He had also made provisions for their escape, if all else failed. The entire fishing fleet and a few Mystrosian ships were positioned around the cape and could be reached quickly in an emergency.

He nodded to himself, satisfied that he had done all that could be done without actually seeing the enemy. He turned to the nearest warrior, a man named Mizzel, who had been one of Braque's favorites when he was king. "Mizzel, I'm going in for a brief rest and a little wine. You're in charge now, so stay alert. If you see a ship, fetch me at once."

Mizzel clicked his heels and bowed. "Yes, sire."

Lord Braque took one last look at the empty horizon and went back into the castle. *A little wine*, he thought, *and maybe a roasted molfrump.*

85

Rhynt sipped at her tea, not sure which story to focus on first. She wanted nothing more than to grab Orthor by the hand, find a quiet place, and listen rapt to his story of runes and Mercadia. That background might serve all of them well in how they dealt with their current predicament: at anchor off an island that could be Mercadia, and certainly a deadly one. Or she could listen to Priss, Phendour, and Blusk recount their harrowing capture by the elves and rescue by Zyrx and Bebo.

She could tell by the way people looked at her that each was bursting with enthusiasm to tell their story in detail. Finally, she asked herself *what would a queen do?*

She cleared her throat. "Gentlemen, each of you comes to table with a story to tell, and all are important to me." She paused to gauge their reaction. She seemed to have their attention. "I assure you, I will spend time with each of you to hear your stories in detail, but for now all of us must focus on the main problem—the elves."

Everyone nodded, and the Red Monk raised his hand.

"Yes?" she said.

"Majesty, to my mind, there are three things we need to discuss: the power of the elves, the surprising attack by the Olasians, and how best to protect Enturia."

Everyone began speaking at once, some in agreement, some in opposition, and some offering new "important things" to discuss.

Rhynt tried to keep up but couldn't. "Stop, all of you."

The voices grew silent.

"Calax, I seemed to hear that you were offering a fourth topic."

"Yes, Majesty, this island itself. We are the only ones in the known world to know its position. That knowledge could be the key to how we react, to everything."

She nodded. "True enough, but it is also a dangerous island. We have no clue why our ships burned or the fate of our men. All we know is that there's a lot of blood and no sign of them."

"Dangerous, yes, but not fully unknown. Before we set out on our rescue, we explored the entire island. It is a lush island with boundless resources."

"But the dangers . . ."

"Admittedly a concern, but one I think we can face now that you, the reinforcements, and Bebo have arrived. Why, Bebo alone will help us face anything dangerous on that island."

"And me, I can help," said a woman's voice.

Everyone looked around, but there was no one there.

"Sorry," said the Red God, appearing by the table. "Now, would you like to hear what I think we should do?"

Calax began to slowly draw his sword, but the Red God held up her hand. "Stop, Calax. I know you think I'm an enemy, and yes, I was once, but there are things afoot you know nothing about and that I cannot in good conscience abide." She looked down at the table. "Is there wine?"

86

Clessus did not like ships. No, not one bit. He much preferred the safety of the Tower, where he had been born and grew up. And, in truth, he did not like Paudia or anything or anywhere in this so-called known world.

But the queen must be obeyed. He said the words out loud, startling another elf standing next to him at the rail.

"Of course, Clessus, of course," the elf said.

Clessus sneered at him. "Don't you have something to do, something that can get us there faster?"

"Yes, sir, sorry, sir," he said, moving away.

Clessus scanned the horizon. The sooner a ship showed up, the sooner he could be back in Paudia in his bed, but there was nothing but waves and a few clouds scudding along in the wind.

He looked back in the direction of Paudia. Nothing, not even a spit of land. The whole idea of being this far from land sent chills down his spine. What if there was a storm? A sea monster—there were many stories of leviathans dragging ships to the bottom and gorging on the crews.

And then the elf he had sent away started yelling and pointing to the northeast. "A ship, a ship."

Clessus squinted at the horizon. It was a ship, and from the look of it, even from this far away, it looked just the way the *Marthe* was described to him.

"Signal the rest of the fleet. We give chase!

87

The Red God pulled up a chair, sat down at the table, and poured herself a glass of Alamarian wine. "I can so use this right about now. You have no idea what I've been through."

Everyone just stared at her as she drained the glass and poured herself another. "What?"

"Why are you here?" said Rhynt. "You abandoned us when we needed you most."

"Orders," she said with a little shrug.

"Orders?"

"From him, the big guy, you know, Randall himself."

"Another god?"

She nodded and took another long drink. "I hope you have more of this. I have a thirst beyond imagination."

"So," said Rhynt, "you're saying there's one god above all the other gods?"

The Red God looked at her like she was crazy. "Of course. Someone has to be in charge, and he's the one."

"So he ordered you to come back to us?"

"No, he ordered me to abandon you in favor of the Mystrosians." She chuckled. "I guess his plan didn't work out."

"So you're here on your own?"

"Yes."

"Why now?"

"Because you'll need a god's help if you set foot on that island out there." She nodded at Orthor. "Just ask him. He knows." She pulled several scrolls out from her shroud and dropped them on the table. "Your scrolls, Orthor. Perhaps you should explain, because I know you know why I'm here."

Everyone looked at Orthor. To Orthor, every eye had a different question.

He cleared his throat and began.

88

It was good to be king, or at least regent, and Lord Braque was enjoying every second of it. People listened to him again, even smiled at him. As obsequious as the smiles were, he took them as a plus.

The meal they had prepared for him was enough for ten people and in great variety, so he lingered at the table, stuffing himself, drinking perhaps a little too much Alamarian wine.

So he was surprised when someone jostled him awake still at table, his head resting on his plate. "What? What is it?"

"Ships, Majesty, coming fast."

Lord Braque focused on the man's face. It was Talbut, a kitchen servant. "Talbut?"

"Yes, Majesty. Hurry, the enemy is approaching."

He yawned. "Enemy?"

"Yes, hurry. We have but an hour at best."

He was finally fully awake. "Yes, yes, of course. Are the men at their stations?"

"I don't know, Majesty. They told me to fetch you, and here I am. You must go, now."

Lord Braque looked at the table. Had he had dessert? The blue cream tarts seemed untouched, and they were his favorite. "All right, go to my chambers and fetch my armor. I'll head to the battlements."

"Yes, Majesty." Talbut bowed and raced from the room.

Lord Braque snagged a tart and ran as fast as he could, which was more like a slow shuffle, his knees screaming, his lungs laboring.

"*A battle*, he thought. *How wonderful!*"

89

Orthor set down his spoon and cleared his throat. "Abo, if you please, the scrolls."

The Red God stood and walked to the end of the table, placing the scrolls in front of him.

He nodded his thanks and began, unrolling the first scroll as he did. "Queen Rhynt, you sent me to the Cave of the Six Arrows and Randall's Cave to solve the mystery of the runes and the paintings that seem to depict you and your hill tigers racing toward a cliff." He paused and looked at her. "I am both happy and fearful to tell you that I have solved both."

"So what does it mean?" said Rhynt. "Is it me, and what exactly are we doing?"

Orthor sighed. "Majesty, it is complicated. If I tell you the answer, you will not have your answer."

"You talk in riddles," she said.

"Majesty, it is a riddle and will remain a riddle unless I begin at the beginning. That is the only way the end will make any sense."

She slumped back in her chair. "Very well." She turned to Marthe. "I suspect we're in for a long night. Could we have more wine and coffee? And perhaps some cakes?"

Marthe pushed back his chair. "I'll see to it." He looked at Orthor. "You may begin your story. I won't be a moment, and besides, I don't like long preambles."

Orthor nodded at him. "Very well."

He turned back to the first scroll, read a bit to remind himself, and began. "It all begins with the destruction of Mercadia by the explosive eruption of its volcano more than a thousand years ago. The island before us is in fact Mercadia, and the harbor where the ships burned is the caldera formed in the eruption's aftermath."

"Are you sure of this?" said Calax.

Orthor didn't hesitate. "Yes, there is no question, as you shall see from the rest of my story."

Rhynt looked around the table. "Please, everyone, hold your questions until the end of Orthor's story. Otherwise, we shall be here until dawn."

Everyone nodded.

"Okay, then, Orthor, continue your story."

"Yes, Majesty." He cleared his throat again. "The person who wrote the runes believed he was the only survivor. He was a fisherman and saw the cataclysm unfold from his small boat a mile or so offshore. Throughout his story, he believes strongly that he was the only survivor, but he does allow for the possibility that others also escaped. Although that is a small hope."

He sat down the first scroll. "And here we come to one of the wonders of the story the runes tell. He mentions a monster, hideous to behold, that dwelled on the island. He calls it the Mercadoo, and wonders whether it survived the blast."

Rhynt gasped. "You mean from the nursery rhyme?"

"Yes, Majesty, but to the writer of the runes, the Mercadoo was no myth to frighten children, but a real, living and breathing monster."

"Okay, okay," she said. "I'm sorry I interrupted. Please continue."

He picked up the second scroll.

90

Clessus stood at the prow of his flagship and squinted at the ship they were following. Was it really the *Marthe?* It looked like the *Marthe* and was certainly fast like the *Marthe*. But he saw no signs of seamanship, no sign of tactics on display. No, the ship was just in headlong, straight-line flight. And Clessus was losing the race.

He called back to the first mate. "More sail. We're losing her."

"Aye, Captain," said the first mate. He screamed at the seamen near him. "More sail."

Twenty elves, seamen all, raced to the task, hoisting an additional sail that seemed to lift the ship out of the water and drag it forward.

Clessus watched the gap closing between his ship and the *Marthe*. "We're gaining. More sail."

"There is no more," said the first mate.

Clessus growled. "Then find more wind."

"We will need the gods for that."

"Then find us a god."

The first mate said nothing, but returned to the task at hand, steering the ship directly at the *Marthe*.

Clessus began pacing and shaking his head. They were gaining on the *Marthe*, but not fast enough. He could already see Enturia on the horizon.

He yelled back at the first mate. "We have to catch them before they reach the Enturian harbor."

The first mate said nothing, but nodded in agreement.

Clessus shook his fist at the *Marthe.* "You bastards, I'll have you before this day is out!"

91

Phendour wasn't sure what to make of Orthor's fantastical story about a monster, but it reminded her of a story her mother used to tell her. She thought there was a monster inside the volcano on Didu, or so she said. Why else would there be so much rumbling and growling. Perhaps it was a fiery dragon or something worse, she had said, from somewhere deep within the earth. Phendour knew in her heart, even then, that her mother was just trying to make sure she stayed away from the volcano.

One thing was certain, thought Phendour. *When the volcano on Didu exploded, it was indeed monstrous.*

She looked over at Ci, the little girl who had tended her shoulder wound. The only thing she seemed interested in was the stack of cakes set down on the table moments earlier. Blusk, who doted on the little girl, waved his hand, encouraging her to snatch a cake, and winked at her when she did.

The others all seemed to be in their own worlds, Orthor's words transporting them to who knows where in their minds. The Red Monk was either asleep or in a trance. Priss was focused on Rhynt and her reactions to Orthor's story. Zyrx was all but asleep, his head nodding down to his chest and then bouncing back up as he tried to recover. Marthe seemed disinterested. He was busy stuffing his pipe with braggus weed, a form of seaweed with the properties of tobacco. Calax's brow was knotted. She had seen that look before. He was calculating what needed to be done the next morning, when they would venture onto Mercadia. Of all of them, Rhynt, Bookins, and the Red God seemed to be taking the monster story the most seriously. All three seemed rapt by Orthor's every word. She wondered what Whelan would think if he was here. *And why isn't he here?* she thought.

Orthor had started speaking again.

"So there's the monster, and we'll get back to it, but the second scroll is mostly a lament about the loss of his family and their former idyllic life on Mercadia."

"We can skip that," said Rhynt. "When do we get to the drawings in The Cave of the Six Arrows?"

"Now, Majesty." He set down the second scroll and picked up the third. "Understand that I was hurried at this point, Majesty, so I only have pieces of what the runes say there."

"Pieces?"

"Um, large pieces, Majesty. Whole sections, but not all."

Rhynt's sigh seemed to fill the room.

"Majesty, what I don't have is descriptions of each of the gods and their powers and—"

"I can help with that," said the Red God. "I know all the gods well."

Rhynt nodded, annoyed at the interruption. "Good, we may have need of that. Now, Orthor, *what else* can't you tell me?"

Orthor hesitated. He knew she would not be pleased. "Um, the actual location of the ravine you seem to be running toward."

Rhynt's eyes went wide. "So the drawing is me and my tigers, sometime in the future?"

"Yes, Majesty, there is no doubt. The names are written in runes there."

Calax interrupted. "And not too far into the future, I would suspect, Majesty. The ravine is here, on this island. I remember the drawing well, and there is no doubt that the ravine is here, not that far into the jungle."

"I thought as much," said Rhynt. She turned back to Orthor. "And do you know why we're running toward the ravine?"

Orthor hesitated.

"Orthor?"

"Majesty."

"What is it?"

He looked around the table. "The runes say you are running to your deaths."

92

Lord Braque stood on the battlements, watching the approach of a fleet of ships. They were still far away, but he could still make out the Enturian fishing boat leading them toward the harbor.

He heard footsteps approaching from behind, so he turned to see who it was. Surprisingly, it wasn't the man he'd sent for his battle armor. It was Cresh, his former manservant, now the servant of Bookins, who had left the man behind to tend to Braque's needs. It was a noble gesture, and Braque greatly appreciated it.

"What do you want?" said Braque.

"You sent a man for your armor, sire, but there is no armor in your chambers."

Braque rolled his eyes. He remembered immediately. After the battle there had seemed no need for armor, so he had taken it to the armory, where other armor and weapons were stored. "Yes, yes, Cresh. Try the armory. I put it there myself."

Cresh hesitated. "I tried the armory, sire, but there is so much armor there, I couldn't find it."

Braque huffed. *Must I do everything myself?* "Very well, come along, and I'll find it for you."

"Yes, sire. Would you like your roller chair?"

Braque smiled at him. "I no longer need it, Cresh. My legs seem to have a new life. So come, and try to keep up."

Braque set off at a fast pace, Cresh trying to keep up.

"We need to make this fast," said Braque. "A fleet approaches, and I'm pretty sure it's our friends the elves coming to claim Enturia as their own."

"We cannot let that happen, sire."

"No, no we can't."

They walked along in silence, finally entering the castle and descending the long flight of steps to the armory.

"Here we are," said Braque, walking up to a set of armor on top of a table. "Right where I left it."

"Yes, sire. Shall I carry it to your chambers or would you like to get into it here."

"Here, of course, no time to dally."

Cresh picked up the breastplate and began strapping it on Braque. "Won't be a minute, sire."

Braque stared around as Cresh did his work. There were piles and piles of shields, stacks of spears, and basket after basket bristling with arrows. And something big in the darkness of a corner. "Here now," he said, "wait a moment. What is that in the corner?"

Cresh stopped strapping Braque into his armor and squinted at the dark corner. "I don't know."

Braque chuckled. "Well, I do."

"Sire?"

"Leave my armor be. What we need now is more men."

"Sire, men? What for?"

"Never mind about that. Go fetch me a dozen men."

"But—"

There was really no need for Braque to shout so angrily, but he did. "Now!"

93

Everyone sat in silence as the meaning of Orthor's words took hold, then Calax slapped his hand down on the table and laughed. "What nonsense!"

Rhynt glared at him. "You think my death funny?"

Calax rolled his eyes. "Majesty, there will be no deaths."

"But the runes . . ."

"Written by a madman in a cave, who knows how many years ago."

Orthor piped up. "Almost a thousand years ago, according to the runes."

"I can confirm that," said Abo. "I have been there many times over the centuries. The runes have been there for as long as I can remember. In fact, now that I think of it, I spoke to the man who put the runes there, and he was no madman. His name was Ramine or some such."

Orthor corrected her. "Ramish."

Abo waved him off. "Whatever."

Rhynt turned to Orthor. "And I and my tigers are mentioned by name. Isn't that right, Orthor?"

"It is, Majesty."

Calax held up a hand. "Even so, Majesty, you need only stay away from the ravine."

She sighed. "Do you think so? Truly?"

"Yes, of course."

"But it is written in stone."

"No," said Abo, "as hard as we gods try—and believe me, we have tried—there is no such thing as fate. The man made a prediction, one based on the input of a god—not me, of course—and that is all. The god hopes that by knowing the prediction, you will feel compelled to act on it."

"That makes no sense," said Rhynt. "Why on earth would a god plan that a thousand years before I was even born? And how would he know my name? And the names of my tigers?"

Abo shrugged. "He likes to play games."

Rhynt was incredulous. "For a thousand years?"

Abo shrugged again. "He likes the long game."

The Red Monk stood up. "Wait, wait, I think we're all asking the wrong question. Why does this god want you to jump to your deaths in the ravine?"

Orthor stood. "I can help with that, I think. The story in the caves ends with her majesty jumping into the ravine. Then the author says, um, wait, let me read it directly from the scroll."

He picked up the scroll. "Yes, yes, here it is. Rhynt and the tigers have jumped into the ravine. Then he says, 'As written in the Mercadicon.'"

"And?" said Rhynt.

"That's it, Majesty. The runes end there."

"So what does that mean?"

"It means the rest of the story can be found in the Mercadicon. Your librarian mentioned it to me once. It is said to contain the complete history of Mercadia, and astoundingly, its future."

Rhynt rolled her eyes. "That's impossible."

Abo shook her head. "Oh, Rhynt, you have no idea what we gods can do when we set our minds to it."

"And this Mercadicon," said the Red Monk. "May we assume it is lost to us now?"

"No," said Orthor. "If this island is indeed Mercadia, it should be part of a vast library in a grand castle."

Calax's eyes went wide. "Library? I have seen it. It is filled to the rafters with books and scrolls."

Rhynt stood. "Then we must find it at first light."

94

Clessus smiled despite himself. They were gaining ground on the *Marthe* with every passing second. With any luck, they would catch the enemy ship before it found safety in Enturia's harbor. His men were already stationed at the prow with grappling hooks, and archers were high on the masts. It would be a quick process, no doubt.

His only concern, and it was a small one, was that the race to capture the *Marthe* had strung out his fleet into a long straight line, with his ship in the lead and the others trailing, though not by much.

He turned to his first mate. "Do you think we should slow down a bit to let the others catch up? I'd much prefer to scare the Enturians by showing our fleet spread across the horizon."

The first mate looked back at the trailing ships, and then turned and looked at the fleeing *Marthe*. "She will make the harbor, though, if we do."

Clessus sighed. "That's what I thought, too."

"Besides," said the mate, "we can take her by ourselves, easy. Then we can spread out and give the Enturians quite a fright."

"Yes, yes, that will work. And I want every man aboard her hanged in the yardarms and the ship set aflame for all to see."

"They will surrender, sure."

"If they know what's good for them, but we'll take them in any event."

The sound of music startled them. A man in bright clothing, a minstrel, was standing behind them, playing a lute. When he saw them gawking at him, he played one last chord and stopped. "I have a suggestion for you, if you don't mind."

95

They launched the longboats at dawn, everyone except Marthe and his crew climbing in the boats as they rocked in the low chop just outside the harbor. Queen Rhynt had suggested that Blusk and Phendour remain behind with Ci to attend to their wounds, but all three had objected. Phendour made the case that she and Blusk were recovering nicely and might be able to help with less strenuous tasks. Ci agreed and said she could tend to their wounds just as easily ashore. Rhynt had relented and let all three climb into her longboat.

The trip to shore took only twenty minutes, and after securing the boats, they set off for the castle, which was a marvel to Rhynt.

"It is so big and grand," she said.

"Wait till you see the inside, Majesty. Though it is near barren of furniture, it is still a wonder." He turned to Orthor. "And you will find the library an even greater wonder."

Orthor smiled. "I can't wait."

"We will go cautiously, though," said Calax.

"The monster?" said Orthor.

Calax said nothing, holding a finger to his lips to silence Orthor, whose eyes went wide as he mouthed the word *what?*

Calax held up a hand and motioned for everyone to stop.

Queen Rhynt came up to him and whispered, "What?"

His reply was swift. "Shh."

She looked around, but saw nothing.

Calax saw her dismay, and whispered as softly as he could. "A rustling, to the left and just ahead."

Rhynt looked but saw nothing. But then she heard it, a low rustling sound coming from the edge of the jungle.

They all took a step back, Calax slowly drawing his sword, followed by Phendour, Blusk, Priss, Zyrx, and Rhynt, all ready and wary.

The Red Monk went into a trance, but then dropped out of it with a laugh. "Ha!"

"What?" said Rhynt.

The Red Monk pointed to his left. "Watch, here it comes."

Seconds later, a molfrump burst from the undergrowth and raced across their path.

Calax was the first to drop his sword at his side. "Well, that's no monster."

A roar came from deep in the jungle, a roar unlike any Calax had ever heard. It was high-pitched, more like a scream, and ended in a rattling and clicking sound.

The Red Monk dropped into a trance again, and dropped out just as quickly again. "To the castle! Quickly!"

They all ran.

96

Lord Braque could see the approaching ships clearly now, and they were positioned just as he had hoped, in a straight line, and coming fast.

The only problem was that they were gaining ground on the Enturian fishing ship, the one he had sent out to lure the fleet in.

Cresh, standing next to him, seemed ready to run. "Sire, what shall we do? They're almost upon us."

"The plan, of course, have you forgotten so soon?"

"But it is just one thing. Will it work against so many ships?"

Lord Braque shrugged. "The ships are not that many. No more than a scouting fleet, if you ask me. They have no intention of attacking us."

"But why would they—"

"Chase our ship? Because they think it's the *Marthe.*"

"But the *Marthe* is—"

"Safely away. We know that, but they don't"

"So we let them take the ship?"

"No, no, no. Our ship must escape to the harbor, so any ship that survives our attack and returns back to Paudia will insist that the *Marthe* is here, in our port."

"I don't understand. Won't that just attract a larger elven force?"

"Yes, yes, of course, but that's the thing, you see."

"No, I don't see."

Lord Braque took a deep breath. Cresh could be so dense at times. "The thing is, Cresh, I don't expect to let any ship escape. They will all be destroyed. Here. Now."

97

Once inside the castle, Calax placed guards at every possible entrance, from the gate, to the dungeons, to the high parapets. There was no reason to believe that the monster could fly, but there was also no reason to believe that it couldn't.

Blood was everywhere, but not a single body was to be found. Whatever had killed the men had clearly dragged their bodies down the steps to the dungeons and out the doorway to the jungle. Queen Rhynt's hill tigers, Mela, Mila, and Spook, paced back and forth, their noses in the air as they frantically searched for a scent they understood. There was something, but what?

Then there was a loud bang at the castle gate, and another, and another. Everyone drew their swords and ran to the gate.

The bang came again and then a voice. "Let in, let in."

Rhynt laughed. "It's Bebo. Let him in."

It took six men to unlock the gate, but only one push by Bebo to bang it open. "Bebo here."

He swung the gate closed again, and the men relocked it.

"Welcome, Bebo," said Rhynt. "I have missed you."

"Me you," he said. "Now joke."

She laughed and pulled him aside, going on tiptoe as he leaned over to listen. A minute later a laugh erupted from him and echoed through the castle. "Good joke. Now another."

Rhynt waggled a finger at him. "Soon, but not yet. First, we'd all like to hear what you found as you swam around this island.

Bebo grunted and sat down on the floor. "Big island. Very big island."

He described high cliffs around most of the island, but a few areas where the land dipped down to the sea forming small, easily accessible harbors. He had gone ashore at one such harbor on the west side of the island and trekked inland through the jungle for several miles.

"Big hole in middle," he said. "Big and long and dark. Me no go."

He had retreated back to the sea and swam on, seeing additional harbors and more and more jungle, as well as birds he had never seen before, before swimming into the atoll where the burned ships still smoldered.

"What about sounds," said Rhynt. "Did you hear a strange roar?"

"Big roar, from big hole."

"The ravine," said Orthor. "From the runes and drawings."

Rhynt nodded. "So it seems."

Bebo tapped her as lightly as he could on the shoulder. "Now joke."

She nodded and put a hand to his ear.

Calax took the opportunity to grab Orthor by the arm. "Come, I'll show you the library."

Orthor didn't need to be asked twice. "Yes, please."

They walked through the grand hall to a small door. "The door is a little stiff," said Calax, putting his shoulder to the door and opening it with a squeak.

Orthor gasped. Even in the low light, he could see scroll after scroll, book after book, in shelves, on the floor, reaching almost to the ceiling. "I will need light, lots of light."

"Of course," said Calax. "There are lanterns every few feet. I'll fetch a flame while you get started."

Orthor walked in, squinting to see any book large enough to be the Mercadicon. The first such volume he saw was an illustrated guide to the flora and fauna of Mercadia. He dusted it off and set it down near the door. He'd give it to Calax when he returned with the flame. Perhaps he could find some mention of the monster.

He moved deeper into the library. There were so many wonders, enough to keep him reading for decades and decades, if he was given the opportunity.

And then he saw it. A large book, two feet tall by one foot wide by six inches thick, sitting open on a table near the library's one window. He closed the book to see the title on its cover. Imprinted in pure gold was a single word: Mercadicon.

His shout echoed through the room.

98

Clessus paced back and forth in front of Whelan as two other elves held the minstrel by his arms.

"I remember you, I think. The minstrel to the queen, correct?"

"Well, there was nothing formal about—"

Clessus stopped and jabbed his finger into Whelan's chest. "You are Whelan the Wanderer."

Whelan chuckled. "Guilty."

"What are you doing here?"

"I thought you'd be setting to sea to catch the *Marthe*, and I have the same goal."

"And yet now you are my prisoner."

Whelan cocked his head. "Yes, that too, but—"

"Take him below and put him in chains."

The guards started wrestling Whelan toward an open hatch, but he resisted. "Don't you want to hear my suggestion?"

"Not particularly."

"Not even if it could help you catch the *Marthe?*"

Clessus laughed and pointed toward the ship they were chasing, which was growing closer and closer. "We are almost upon her. I need no help."

"Oh, but you do."

Clessus rolled his eyes. "And why is that?"

"Because that ship you're chasing is not the *Marthe*."

"Not the *Marthe?* Don't be ridiculous."

"Ha! You want to know what's ridiculous? It's you, trying to explain to Queen Daneyh how you were fooled by an old man."

Clessus glanced at the fleeing ship and then. "You mean Bookins? Another of his gambits."

Whelan laughed. "No, even worse. The old king, Braque, the laughing stock of the Battle of the Plain of Sorrows."

Clessus gulped.

99

It seemed to Orthor that there were now more people in the library than books. Everyone had rushed in at his shout, some sensing the excitement in his voice, others sensing something else, a scream fitting for the presence of a monster. So the first group had smiled at him, delighted by his find, and the second group had rolled their eyes and frowned, thinking that they were the victims of a cruel joke.

Orthor clutched the book to his chest. "I have found it—the Mercadicon."

"I would read it first," said the Red God.

"No," said Rhynt. "I shall." She looked at Orthor. "With Orthor."

"And *me*," said the Red God with a force that suggested she would not be denied.

Calax stepped forward. "Is it in runes?"

"No," said Orthor, "the common tongue."

"Then perhaps one of you can read it to all of us. We all have an interest in knowing more about this island—and whatever monster resides here."

Orthor nodded. "I can do that."

"Or perhaps we can take turns," said the Red God.

"Yes, that makes sense," said Rhynt.

"Then let's move to the throne room. There are enough chairs there to accommodate us, as well as a table where Marthe's cook can provide us with food and drink."

"Is there a throne?" said Rhynt.

"Yes," said Calax. "But would you really sit on another's throne?"

Rhynt groaned. "Of course not, but it would make an ideal location for the reader, with the rest of us gathered round."

"Sounds good to me," said Orthor with a smile. "It will be my only taste of being royalty."

Rhynt laughed. "I wouldn't be so sure of that, Sir Orthor."

Orthor blinked. "What?"

"Kneel," she said, then turned to Calax. "Your sword, sir."

Calax drew his sword and handed it to her.

"And now," she said, "I dub you Sir Orthor Billibuck, knight of the realm, second librarian of Enturia, first librarian proper of Mercadia, and counselor to the queen." She tapped the sword on his left shoulder and then his right. "Rise now, sir knight."

Orthor tried to get out words, but words didn't come.

"Save your words, and your voice, for later," she said, "when you sit upon the throne and enthrall us with your story."

Orthor stood and bowed. "Majesty."

She reached out her hand. "Come, Orthor, we have a lot of reading to do." She turned to the others. "Come now, all of you."

100

Lord Braque could not disguise his delight at the scene unfolding in front of him. Their fishing ship was just outside the harbor and coming on fast. There was no question that it would make it to the safety of the Enturian harbor. The trailing fleet, clearly captured Mystrosian ships manned by elves, was coming close behind, straight and true, right into the sights of a crossbow intended for a forest troll as tall as a tree.

He and his men had lashed it to the wharf, pointing it directly out to sea. Twelve men had cranked its large sharp bolt, more than the length of three men and thick as a leg, to its sticking point. All that was needed now was for two men with large mallets to strike the trigger and loose the bolt.

Braque watched the oncoming ships carefully. He wanted them to come a little closer before he loosed the first bolt, to do as much damage as possible. But not too close. He also wanted to get off a second shot and perhaps a third, enough to scatter the ships and send them back where they came from.

Cresh broke him from his reverie. "Sire, the ships," he shouted. "They're turning."

Braque looked at the ships in horror. "No, no, no!"

He ran toward the men with the mallets. "Loose, loose, loose!"

The men acted quickly, raising their mallets and bringing them down hard on the trigger. The whole wharf shook from the recoil of the crossbow as it sent the bolt flying toward the fleet.

The reading went on for hours, each reader given the honor of sitting on the throne, as the others, gathered round close to the throne, listened with rapt attention. Food was brought in and placed on a row of tables gathered from all over the castle. Some tables were high and some were low, giving the food the look of a mountain range.

Calax seemed impatient, interrupting several times to request that the reader skim ahead to find any mention of the monster. Queen Rhynt had chastised him each time. "Please stop interrupting. We will get to the monster in due course."

Calax's response each time had been some variant of, "I hope we get to the monster before he gets to us."

After the first two hours, Queen Rhynt suggested a break, so that everyone could eat a proper meal and see to their personal needs, a suggestion roundly applauded by the rest.

Zyrx then pulled Calax aside. "You keep interrupting. Why don't you just read the book Orthor gave you, on the flora and fauna of the island?"

"I don't know what flora and fauna is. Sounds boring."

Zyrx gave him a look.

"What?"

"You really don't know what flora is, or fauna?"

"Sounds like girls' names."

Zyrx chuckled. "Oh, Calax. No, not girls' names, though Flora would serve. No, flora means plants and such, and fauna means animals and such."

Calax looked stunned. "Animals? So maybe . . ."

"So maybe, yes, it could have a drawing of the beast."

Calax looked around the room. "Where did I put it? Ah, there it is."

He ran for the book.

102

Lord Braque watched in horror as the ships turned to the north, away from Enturia. The first bolt flew by the first six ships and grazed the mast of the seventh.

He screamed at his men. "To the right."

They adjusted the crossbow, nocked the bolt, and fired again, the second bolt striking the third ship in the line and cutting it in two. But all the others were getting away at full sail.

"One more, men."

They complied, sending their last bolt into the air toward the first of the fleeing ships. Braque watched its flight, then groaned as the bolt missed the first ship and flew off in the direction of Paudia.

Braque dropped to his knees. "We are undone."

Cress pulled him to his feet. "No, sire, we are made. The ships flee. Enturia is safe. And we have taken out one of their ships, at least."

Braque took a deep breath. "It is as you say, but now our queen is at risk. They head in the direction of Mercadia."

Cress laughed. "Mercadia? No, sire, that is a myth. There is no such place."

Braque shook his head. "Oh, Cress. There is much I must tell you. Mercadia is real, and if I am not mistaken, our queen is there now, helping Calax and the others."

"But sire."

"No, Cress, I will say no more now. We have two tasks before us, and they need our attention now."

"Tasks?"

"We must send a bird, no two, to warn the queen."

"And the second?"

"I have another idea, Cress."

"What, sire?"

"Come, I'll explain it on our way to the pigeons."

103

Everyone gathered around Calax as he flipped quickly through the pages of the flora and fauna book, drawings of strange plants and animals flying by as he searched for anything resembling a monster. The only thing close was a saber-toothed molfrump no bigger than a rabbit. It looked fierce, but there was no way it could have taken down a grown man and dragged him away.

Calax dropped the book to the floor. "Nothing."

"Wait a minute," said Phendour, picking up the book. "You went too fast. It has to be here."

She moved slowly through the book, and then sighed. "Here, look, someone has torn out several pages."

"Orthor," said Rhynt. "Was there any mention of the monster in the cave runes?"

"Yes, but only the name, the Mercadoo."

"No description?"

"No."

She shook her head. "Then let's hope there's something in the Mercadicon. Orthor, it's your turn to read again. Are you ready?"

Orthor cleared his throat. "Yes."

He walked back to the throne, picked up the heavy book, and opened it to the place Priss had left off.

There were in those days strange rumblings from the volcano. The ground would shake and smoke would rise, but these times were few and infrequent. Then, in the year of King Plazco's ascent to the throne, the ground shook more violently, opening up great chasms in the earth, ripping the ground like it was no more than the sheerest cloth. And then, as the ground grew quiet, we heard the roar that in the days to come would frighten us to our cores. The Mercadoo was among us.

104

Whelan crossed his arms and smiled at Clessus. "So you see, you were wise to take my, um, suggestion."

Clessus nodded. "It is as you say."

"Otherwise . . ."

"We would all be at the bottom of the sea. I know that, and I thank you for your advice."

"I have more if you've a mind to listen."

"Of course."

Of course. Whelan liked the sound of that. "Well, then, you need only change course slightly to the east and you shall have your prize."

"The *Marthe?*"

Whelan chuckled. "Oh, that—*and more.*"

"More?"

"Indeed. You will have the *Marthe,* and Marthe himself, plus Calax Halfhand, Queen Rhynt, Zyrx, Phendour, Blusk, Bebo the troll, a harem girl named Ci, and all the others that have joined them on Mercadia."

Clessus's eyes had gone wide and wider with each name, but dropped to a squint when Whelan mentioned Mercadia. Whelan saw the look. "Believe me, it is as real as you or I, and we can capture them all there. We outnumber them and we will have the element of surprise. Just think how pleased your queen will be. By taking their queen, you take Enturia as well."

Clessus couldn't help smiling. She would be more than pleased. There would be gold for him and a promotion. "How far away?"

Whelan looked up at the sun. "We will be there by dawn. A perfect time, don't you think?"

105

Finally, it was Bebo's turn to read, but he just shook his head. "Me no read. See funny squiggles, is all."

"Then I shall go again," said Queen Rhynt.

Ci had another idea. "Majesty, if I may. You skipped over me, and I can read as well as anyone here."

Rhynt raised an eyebrow. "I did not know. I thought harem girls were forbidden that skill."

Ci nodded. "It is true, but a eunuch saw my interest in books." She turned to Bebo. "And those little squiggles. And taught me how to read, just as I will help you read, Bebo."

Bebo beamed. "No joke?"

"No joke, but I will teach you how to read jokes."

Now his eyes grew wide. "There is such a thing? Jokes hidden in squiggles."

Ci laughed. "Yes, and I'm sure we'll find such a book in the library here."

"And if not," said Bookins, "I have one back in Enturia."

Bebo sniffed, fighting back tears of joy. "Good books, good friends."

"Now, Ci, if you please," said Rhynt. She motioned her toward the throne and the open book. "It is time."

Ci moved to the throne, climbed up, and placed the open book on her lap. She looked around the room. Everyone was watching her, eager to have her begin. So she did.

The monster came at night, sparing no one. Not the lame, not the sick, not even babes in their cribs. No one saw it the first few nights. There was just a stain of blood across the floors, down the steps, and into the jungle. But then a guard caught sight of it as it carried a victim in its maw. It was huge and hairy and seemed to have more mouth than head. Its teeth were long and sharp, and it grasped its victim with four long tentacles not unlike those of the octopus, but red and slimy.

Ci shuddered. "A moment." She wiped away a tear, and began again.

Its eyes, which seemed to embody anger, were as blue as fresh-calved ice, and once they fixed on their target, they never looked away.

"Wait," said Rhynt. "What does that mean, *fresh-calved ice?*"

"It is very cold in the north, miles and miles north of Ichthia," said the Red God "The ice there is wide and thick, taller even than the tallest trees in the South. And at times, when the air warms, large blocks break off. They are referred to as calves, I do not know why."

"Thank you, Abo. I did not know that, but having never been there, I cannot imagine what kind of blue that is."

Abo smiled. "Of course you couldn't. It is the very lightest of blues. Think of the sky, but much lighter, a color barely there."

"So the eyes could be seen even in low light?"

Abo blinked. This girl was smart. "Yes, exactly."

"Good, so we have our first weakness. We must remember that." She nodded at Ci. "You may continue."

Ci looked down at the book. "So . . ."

Its legs, which also were covered by dark brown hair, were long and thin, and ended with three-toed webbed feet the color of orange clay. Each toe was tipped with a long claw that could hold a victim fast or rip their body in half.

Ci looked up from the book. "The description ends here."

"A formidable opponent," said Calax.

"Yes," said Rhynt. She looked around the room. "I suggest we stop here and get ready for what might come this night. Calax, would you see to the defenses?"

"Yes, Majesty." He stood and walked toward the door. "Phendour, Blusk, Zyrx . . . to me."

"And me," said Ci, setting the book down on the throne and chasing behind them. "Where Phendour and Blusk go, I go."

106

They tried their best to block every entrance to the castle, but there were more ways in than they had men to guard them. In the end, they had left several small openings unblocked to focus on the larger, and most likely, entrances for the beast.

Everyone was in the castle, including the crews from the ships. They didn't want a repeat of the carnage they had seen in the harbor upon their arrival. The castle seemed the safer place.

Satisfied with their work, Calax and the others returned to the throne room to report to Queen Rhynt.

"Majesty, everyone is within the castle walls, and we have done our best to block and guard the most likely entrances for the beast."

The queen corrected him. "Beasts."

"What?"

"We kept reading in your absence. It is not one beast, but many."

"How many?"

"Unknown," said Orthor. "The text refers to a horde in one place and to a colony in another. Suffice to say, there are more than one."

Calax took a deep breath. "No, wait, if there was a horde, as you say, wouldn't they have eaten everything on this island already? I mean, the island is alive with all manner of species, who seem to be thriving."

Orthor nodded. "I thought the same thing, so perhaps the number of beasts is not as great as the text suggests."

"How old is that text?"

"Over a thousand years old."

"Stranger still. Perhaps they hibernate like cave bears, and we have roused them from their slumber."

"The text suggests they are night hunters, so perhaps the other animals have figured out a way to avoid them."

"Holed up like us, you mean? said Rhynt.

"Yes," said Orthor.

"Maybe," said Rhynt, "but one thing is clear to me. We will need torches and fires to keep them at bay."

"Yes," said Calax. "I will see to it."

Rhynt started to reply, but the sound of distant roars filled the room.

"I will hurry, Majesty. Night is almost upon us."

"Good." She turned to Abo, the Red God. "Is there nothing you can do to protect us?"

"I will try my best, but I think you should know that another god, or gods, may be at work here, so my powers might not be enough."

"The gods depicted on the cave wall, you mean."

"Yes, and one other, the God of Gods, Randall Himself."

"Randall?"

"You may know him as Whelan the Wanderer."

Rhynt's eyes went wide.

107

The night had gone well. The wind was at their back, billowing the sails, pushing them faster and faster toward Mercadia. If anything, Clessus was worried that they would arrive too soon and be spotted by the Enturians.

Whelan, however, counseled otherwise. "No need to worry. I am already adjusting the winds. We will arrive just after dawn, and no earlier. The important thing is for your other ships to perform as you've told them."

"The arc?"

"Yes, not a straight line and not broadside to the beach."

"Pointed straight in, as you said, to avoid making a good target for whatever weapons they have."

"Exactly. If they have such a weapon as the one we faced in Enturia, we will be ready."

"I hope you are right."

"I am a god, am I not? All will go well, and if there is a surprise—and I expect none—I will handle it. Now, what is your first objective?"

"Their ships."

"Exactly, we want them to have no means of escape."

"So we surround them, board them, and scuttle them."

"Understand that it won't be easy. I know Marthe and the *Marthe* well, as I do its crew. They are fierce fighters, particularly when they're cornered. And with Calax Halfhand on board, victory will come at a great cost."

Clessus nodded. "My elves will take them. I am sure of it."

Whelan smiled, and the ship sailed on through the night.

108

The night had not gone well. The roars of the Mercadoos had grown louder and louder as the sun set, and finally ended in one great roar that struck terror into all of them. And then the Mercadoos attacked, trying their best to break through the defenses that Calax had set up with the others.

He, Phendour, and Blusk had raced from entrance to entrance, helping the men stationed there to rebuff the beasts. Calax and Blusk swung their swords, lopping off tentacle after tentacle, while Phendour shot arrow after arrow into the heads and chests and mouths of the monsters.

But as the hours passed, the Mercadoos breached entrance after entrance, dragging many men into the darkness to their deaths, roars and screams now equal in number.

Finally, Calax ordered everyone to the throne room, which was more easily defended. Half their original number made it into the room before the doors were closed and barricaded. Then, there was nothing to do but wait and hope that the Mercadoos would grow tired and leave.

The roars and pounding continued for two more hours, the barricades holding. Rhynt's hill tigers roared back in defiance. Then, as the first rays of light streamed into the high windows, everything grew quiet except for the collective sigh of relief from those who had survived the night.

Calax was the first to sheath his sword. The others took that as a signal and did likewise, each nodding at Calax and then shaking their heads, wondering how they had survived the night.

109

The pigeons arrived with the morning light, each carrying the same warning: the elves are coming. And coming fast. Rhynt and Calax were the first to see them, small sails on the horizon, but even that far away, they could tell a formidable force was coming, one far greater in number than theirs, which had already been reduced by half after just one night.

"We will have to flee," said Rhynt. "They are too many."

"Aye," said Calax. "And the sooner, the better."

"Let's go tell the others."

They turned and walked back into the castle. The news was met with relief by everyone but Orthor. "What of the library? Those priceless books and scrolls?"

"Take them," said Rhynt. "As many as you can, but quickly."

Marthe stepped up. "We have an extra longboat now, so use that."

"And I will help you load them, too," said Bebo.

"Thank you," said Orthor. "Thank you all." He turned to Bebo. "Let's get to it."

"And hurry," said Rhynt, again. "You have but an hour, and then we must go."

Orthor nodded and ran for the library, along with Bebo, who bounded past him.

Rhynt locked at the others. "I am glad we are leaving. I would have made the same decision even without an enemy fleet on the horizon."

"As would I," said Calax.

"And I," said the Red God. "This is all the work of Randall. The monsters, the elves, all of it. If anything, I think we should abandon the books. Our time is very short."

"No," said Rhynt, "we will save the books, and leave the rest to the Mercadoos. Okay, everyone, let's get busy."

110

Whelan looked in every direction as he paced the deck. "Where are they?"

Clessus raised an eyebrow. "Who?"

"My fellow gods, of course."

Clessus blinked. "There are more?"

"Yes, six more, and they're all late, very late."

"What would you have them do?"

Whelan waved his hand. "That is not for you."

"But—"

"No, you need to pay attention now. Your ships approach Mercadia, and you must prevent their escape. All will die. All."

"But I was instructed to capture them, not kill them. My queen shall decide their fate."

Whelan scoffed. "Their fate? How absurd. I have already decided the fate of each and every one of them. Their deaths will be excruciating, each a masterpiece of pain and dismemberment."

"But the queen—"

"Will have to be satisfied with victory, total victory. Now go, leave me, tend to your duties."

Clessus backed away, then turned and walked back to the wheel of the ship, giving orders as he went.

Whelan resumed his pacing. *Where were they? He had given them strict instructions about time and place and their roles in the coming battle. Had they forgotten? Or was something more sinister at work.*

A shape on the east horizon caught his attention. He squinted at first, then went into a trance, and far-seed.

No, no, no!

"Clessus!"

III

Lord Braque spotted the elven fleet, and snorted. "We outnumber them."

Cresh shook his head. "Yes, but we are only fishing boats, manned by mostly fishermen."

"They will have to do. I couldn't leave Enturia unguarded, now could I?"

"No, but these men, they know about hooks and nets, but *this?*" He pointed at the immense crossbow that had been mounted to the prow of the ship. "This is beyond them."

Braque scoffed. "It is nothing more than lifting, cranking, and swinging a mallet. Anyone could do it."

"But they must do it *well.* Without practicing."

"I'm not worried. Even if they miss five times out of six, we will win."

"But—"

"And we have three ships equipped with crossbows, and plenty of bolts to carry the day."

Cress shook his head. There was no way to dissuade Lord Braque. "As you say, sire."

"Good, now find the signalman for me. We need to notify the other ships to follow my lead with the first crossbow."

"Signalman?"

"Yes, you know, the man who . . ." His voice dropped off.

"Signals, yes, but they are all back in Enturia."

Braque sighed. "There must be someone. Bring this ship's captain to me, now."

Cress nodded and moved toward the stern of the ship.

Braque stared at the enemy fleet, which seemed to be turning to face them.

Was this really going to work?

112

Whelan pounded his fists on the rail. "So annoying."

His plan to take Mercadia in one swift move was dashed. Now he had to turn his fleet, or at least part of it, to deal with Lord Braque. He had seen the crossbows and what they could do when they hit their target. And he didn't want to be that target.

"Clessus, we need to steer this ship and at least six others to face this oncoming fleet."

Clessus chuckled. "But they're just fishing boats."

Whelan rolled his eyes. "With crossbows. Do you remember those crossbows?"

Clessus gulped. "Yes."

"Well, they have three of them now."

"But what about the island?"

"It will be there. We have them trapped, so just position the rest of our ships in a line across the harbor."

"Aye, that makes sense."

"Of course it does. Now, signal the ships and let's take care of those fishing boats."

Clessus nodded and walked away, grabbing a seaman by the arm as he went.

Whelan turned back to the fishing boats, who were growing closer and closer. He knew exactly what to do. He would move some of the ships as if he were going to face them, while he created two waves, one from the north and one from the south, to sink them before they got into range.

He had to smile.

113

Bebo, Orthor, and the others gathered the books as quickly as they could and loaded them into their two longboats. Bebo then waded into the water, dragged them to the *Marthe*, and dumped the books out on the deck before returning for another load. But with only an hour to work with and the elven fleet growing closer and closer, Bebo was only able to make two trips to the *Marthe* with the longboats. On the next trip, they would have to leave the remaining books, which still numbered in the hundreds, and ferry everyone back to the ship.

But they had miscalculated.

"Too close," said Bebo, pointing at the array of approaching ships. "Too late."

"He's right," said Marthe. "They'll have us surrounded before we can make sail."

"Aye," said Calax. "We're trapped."

"So what now?" said Rhynt.

"Wait," said Blusk, pointing out to sea. "Are those our fishing boats?"

Everyone squinted at the boats, then Rhynt dropped into a trance to far-see. "They are, and I can see Lord Braque in the lead ship. And something else. They have some sort of device lashed to the prow. If I'm not mistaken, it's a crossbow, the kind Zyrx made for the forest trolls."

She dropped out of the trance. "They are attacking the elven fleet."

The Red God, who had been watching the approach of both fleets, shook her head. "Their attack will fail."

"How do you know?" said Rhynt. "The crossbow is a formidable weapon. A single bolt could take down a ship."

"Look again, to the north and the south."

Rhynt dropped back into her trance, then gasped. "Waves, giant waves. Lord Braque is doomed."

"As are we, then," said Calax. "Look, half their fleet is still coming at us, and fast."

"We'll never reach my ship in time," said Marthe.

Bebo laughed, a booming laugh that startled all of them.

"What's so funny?" said Rhynt.

"Me have idea."

"What?"

"You flee. Through castle. Down steps. Into Jungle. To other side of island."

"I don't understand. What good will that do?"

Bebo suppressed a giggle. "Me drag ships around island. Meet you at little harbor."

"But there are too many ships."

"Not for Bebo. Me pull fast."

"He's right," said the Red God. "And with us still on the beach, at least for a time, they won't pursue him."

"They'll come for us, though," said Calax.

"Yes," said the Red God, "but if we time it right, this could work."

Rhynt sighed. "But what about the Mercadoos?"

Phendour looked at the sun. "It is early morning. We should be able to make it across the island before dark."

"Aye," said Calax, "but we'll have to move fast."

"Me move fast now," said Bebo, "but need one thing."

"What?" said Rhynt. "A joke?"

"Yes," said Bebo. "But not now. At little harbor. When everyone safe."

Rhynt smiled at him. "Deal."

Bebo laughed and splashed into the water.

Calax, the Red God, and the Red Monk stayed behind on the docks to do whatever they could to slow the pursuit of the elves, Calax to wield his sword and the other two to wield their powers. Bebo had been right. He was too fast for the approaching ships and could barely be seen now as he tugged the two ships around the cape.

"He's made it," said Calax. "They'll never catch him now."

"Yes," said the Red Monk. "They've turned away from him and are heading for us now." He turned to the Red God. "What do you suggest?"

The Red God stared out to sea. "We need to delay them as best we can until the others arrive."

"Others?" said Calax.

"The gods, my fellow gods. If they come at all."

"What do you mean?" said the Red Monk.

"Whelan, Randall himself, has called them, and so have I."

"So you're calling for a mutiny," said Calax.

The Red God nodded. "If they come, yes. If not, I will be an outcast, and he will come for me with a vengeance."

"Or all of you with a vengeance," said Calax.

"Exactly," said the Red God. "But as powerful as he is, our numbers would be a match for him."

The Red Monk pointed at the fishing fleet. "I can put more wind in their sails, so they can outrace the waves."

"No," said the Red God. "I'll take the waves and the elven ships approaching Lord Braque's. You take the ships approaching us. Take the wind out of their sails."

"And I'll . . . " Calax began.

The Red God laughed. "And you'll watch."

Cresh was the first to see the waves, and screamed.

Lord Braque shook his head. *Was this man afraid of everything? How can I aim the crossbow with him screaming in my ears?* "What is it now, Cresh?"

"Waves, sire," he said, "coming in two directions."

Braque's head was on a swivel, looking at both waves and the speed of their rise. "By the gods!"

"It can only be so," said Cresh. "We must turn away, now."

"No, we will have time for at least two rounds of three before the waves reach us."

But—"

"And then we'll have to swim for the shore."

"But—"

"You can't swim. I know that. And neither can I, but I will not let them win."

"But—"

"Not ever. Now shut up and signal the other ships. They should fire after we fire." He raced down the deck to the crossbow and the men busy nocking the bolt. "Faster!"

They moved faster and the bolt was cranked to the sticking point.

"Faster!"

They moved faster and the men with the hammers struck the huge trigger.

"Away! Reload!"

Whelan's eyes grew wide as the first bolts hit the fleet. One bolt caught a ship broadside and sliced it in two. A second bolt hit the mast of another ship and sliced it in two, the ship rolling on its side.

And now his ship was rocked by a third bolt. It hit the ship at the water line and passed through the ship, breaking through on the other side. The ship shuddered and began to sink, elves jumping overboard to save themselves.

Whelan stood there on the sinking ship, shaking his head and looking at the waves he had created. Something was wrong. They should have been taller and faster. But if anything, they were shrinking and slowing.

He sensed the source of the magic and turned to face it.

The Red God could feel her powers being countered, and from the moans coming from the Red Monk, she knew he, too, was having trouble maintaining his charm. Whelan was just too powerful.

Calax, who had been watching the progress of the fishing fleet, cheered when he saw the crossbow bolts strike home, but looked on in horror as the waves smashed into their little fleet, sinking most of them instantly. "By the gods!"

The Red God and the Red Monk broke from their trances.

"It is too much for me," said the monk, dropping to his knees.

"And me," said the god.

"Well, we have to do *something*," said Calax. "Lord Braque is out there, and he may be drowning."

"There is no time," said the god. "And now the elven ships are heading for shore. We need to leave and catch up with the others."

"But I owe my life to that man."

The god sighed. "Let me see what I can see." He dropped back into a trance, and then out of it just as quickly. "He is alive, clinging to the mast of his ship."

"Then let's get him."

"Yes," said the monk, standing. "Surely, you must have some charm that will lift him out of the water and bring him to us."

"Oh, very well," said the god.

Lord Braque clung to the mast for dear life and frantically searched for Cress, but it was soon clear that the seas had taken him. The water was cold, so cold, and he could feel himself losing his grip on the slippery wood.

He tried his best to hold on, but couldn't. He lost his grip and slipped into the water. *I am doomed*, he thought, as the water came over his head and he was forced to hold his breath. *My ploy didn't work, and I have sent men to their deaths. It is only fitting that I die with them.*

He opened his mouth to let the water in, to end it all here and now. Take one last deep breath and then . . .

He was flying through the air.

116

Rhynt and her hill tigers led the way, followed single file by Orthor, Bookins, Priss, Phendour, Blusk, Zyrx, Marthe, Ci, and what was left of the crews from the two ships. At first there was a path, and their progress was swift, but the path soon disappeared, the jungle growing thicker, slowing their progress, each step a fight against the undergrowth.

Finally, Priss moved to the front and began hacking at the vines and plants that blocked their way. She shouted back to Zyrx. "I think these vines are tougher than your merilium."

Everyone laughed, and it felt good to break the tension. There were monsters out there after all, and although they had attacked at night, everyone had the same thought: *what if they attacked now.*

Zyrx laughed the heartiest of all. "My merilium is stronger!"

"Well," said Priss, "I could use a few more merilium swords up here, if anyone would care to give me a hand."

"Me," said Rhynt, drawing her sword.

"Me, too," said Ci with a giggle.

"And me," said Phendour.

"And me," said Blusk.

"But what about your shoulder injuries?" said Zyrx.

"I still have one good arm," said Phendour.

"As do I," said Blusk. He moved to the front, then turned to Zyrx. "What about you? You have a sword?"

"I am too short. I would chop you off at the ankles."

Everyone laughed again, then set about hacking and chopping their way through the vines.

And then someone screamed.

117

Whelan could see them clearly on the docks—the Red God, her monk, and Calax Halfhand. He turned to Clessus and pointed at the docks. "To the longboats. We have them!"

Clessus, who was already up to his knees in water in the sinking ship, nodded. "Aye, sounds like a good idea."

He gave a shout to his men, and the longboats were lowered into the water, the elves scrambling to get in before the ship keeled over and sank. Whelan was the last to climb aboard.

"To the oars!" he shouted, and the elves dutifully picked up the oars and began rowing for shore.

But rowing hard would not be quick enough. Whelan could see Calax and the others running toward the castle, with Lord Braque following much more slowly. He dropped into a trance, and the longboats immediately lurched forward, picking up speed by the second.

Calax turned back to encourage Lord Braque forward, but age and the battle had already stolen the old man's ability to move faster than a shuffle. "Come, we must go," he shouted.

But Lord Braque just stopped and bent over, trying to catch his breath. "It is no use. Leave me. Save yourselves."

"Nonsense," said Calax. He ran back to him, and lifted him into the air.

"What are you doing?"

"Giving you a ride."

"But that will slow you down."

The Red God ran up to them. "He is right. Put him down. I have another idea."

"What?"

"Come," she said. She turned and motioned her monk forward. "You, too. Come, let us join hands. Hurry, form a circle. Hold hands."

They formed a circle and held hands, each looking at the other, not sure what she planned to do.

"Now," she said. "Take a deep breath and close your eyes."

A second later, they all vanished.

Lord Braque screamed as he materialized with Calax, the monk, and the Red God, all the others in the clearing startling, some even screaming in reaction.

"That was something," said Braque, smiling. "Can we do that again?"

"Let's hope that's not necessary," said the Red God. She turned to Queen Rhynt. "Your Majesty, the elves are coming ashore in great number. We need to move, quickly."

Queen Rhynt nodded. "Yes, of course. We're just resting a bit in this clearing before making our way along the edge of the ravine and back into the jungle." She looked up at the sun. "We still have hours before dark. We'll be fine."

"No," said the Red God. "You've made a path for those following. They will be upon us faster than you realize."

Rhynt looked around at the others, who were nodding at the Red God's words. "Very well, let's go."

"No, wait," said Orthor, running farther into the clearing. "Come see."

Orthor now stood next to what looked like a circular stone table, partially covered in vines and weeds. "Help me clear this off."

Everyone tore at the vines, some shouting in wonder at what lay beneath.

"I can't believe it," said Orthor.

"What?" said Rhynt.

"Runes. Hundreds of runes."

Whelan, Clessus, and the survivors of the other ships made their way to shore in the charmed longboats, and began moving toward the castle.

"We will find no one there," said Whelan.

"So we stay in the castle?"

Whelan raised an eyebrow. "Are you that dense?"

"Well, you said—"

"I said nothing about staying in the castle." He looked at the elves straggling up the beach, and stopped. "Get your warriors organized. Send a third east along the shore and another third west. The last third—the best of them—go with us through the castle and into the jungle. I think I know exactly where they're heading, but you can never tell what that imp Bookins might come up with."

"Aye," said Clessus, turning back toward the men.

Whelan began running toward the castle. He knew no one would be there, so he thought of more troubling things. He could not understand why the other gods had not yet arrived. Calling for them, searching for them had been futile. Something was up with them. But what?

He stopped and looked up at the castle, which had weathered badly since the last time he was here, eons and eons ago, when Mercadia was thriving. He had warned them about the volcano, but they hadn't listened. He had told them about the Mercadoos, but they hadn't listened.

"Fools!"

120

Orthor climbed up on the low circular stone table to get a better look. The runes were divided into six equal sections, each divided by thin bands of plain rock. Another band near the center formed a circular area, and this too was covered with runes. His eyes went wide. "I know what this is."

"What?" said Queen Rhynt.

"The drawings, in the cave, of the six gods."

"Yes?"

"Surely, you remember. They were standing on this table, or platform, or whatever we should call it."

"It is true," said the Red God.

"So what is it?" said Rhynt.

The Red God hesitated. "Um . . ."

"Come on," said Rhynt. "What is it? What is it for?"

The Red God sighed. "It is the Summoning Stone."

"Which is . . ."

"A way to summon a god or gods."

"I don't understand."

The Red God sat down on the edge of the table. "This is my section. To summon me, you would only need to decipher the runes and say them out loud."

"But anyone could summon you?"

She nodded. "Even now. You see, when the world was young, we gods were more involved with ordinary people. The Mercadians, the first people, were our friends and wards. If they needed help, they could call on us for help. And we were compelled to provide it."

"Compelled?"

"By Whelan the Wanderer, Randall himself, God of Gods. That center section is his."

"So they could call him directly?"

The Red God snorted. "Oh, no. All gods are lazy—I hated to be summoned—but Whelan was, is the laziest of all. No, only we could call him, after the people had called us, and most important, only after all six gods had been called. Then and only then could Whelan be summoned."

Orthor chuckled. "Sounds like he is very lazy."

"He is, or rather, was. Now he is intent on reshaping the entire world." The Red God turned to Rhynt. "And his intent is to kill you, here, now."

Rhynt shuddered. "But why?"

The Red God shrugged. "I don't know. He is not a big thinker, so it is probably something petty. At any rate, it's not all that important at this point. He is coming for you. I can see him in the jungle now, and he can see us." She paused and looked around at them. "Do you trust me?"

Queen Rhynt wasn't sure what to say. "I'm not sure, really. Back at the Battle of Plain of Sorrows, you seemed to be against us."

The Red God nodded. "I abandoned you, that's true, but now I see Whelan for what he is, a demented god, a god who must be taken down."

"But he is the most powerful."

"Yes, but he can't stand against all six of us."

Bookins stepped forward. "The gods—the other gods—they feel the same as you do?"

"Yes," said the Red God. "And rather than waste any more of our precious time, we should summon them." She turned to Orthor. "Would you do the honors?"

Orthor smiled, eager to help. "Of course."

He walked up to the first section of the stone table. "Oh, this one's yours. Do I need to summon you?"

"It sounds strange, but yes." She waved her hand, encouraging him to begin.

Orthor looked at the runes and translated. "By the power of the gods and the needs of the people, I summon Abo, the Red God, for I am in need."

Abo immediately dematerialized and rematerialized standing in her section of the stone. "Go on, do the others."

Orthor went from section to section, summoning each god in turn: Porto the White, Canto the Blue, Bedo the Green, Dado the Gray, and Indo the Black. Each materialized, looked around, and laughed as if they had been invited to a party.

"What about Whelan?" said Orthor.

"Oh, no, no, no," said the Red God. "Not yet."

She looked around at her fellow gods. "Thank you for coming."

"Did we have a choice, Abo?" said Indo the Black with a laugh.

The Red God smiled. "No, no you did not. But I have to ask each of you now, are you prepared to do this, to bring Whelan's reign to its end?"

All the gods seemed to speak at once.

"Yeah, I've had it with him," said Porto.

"Of course, I'll be happy to be rid of him," said Canto.

"He's too hands-on, so yeah," said Bedo.

"Absolutely yes," said Dado.

"I can't wait," said Indo.

The Red god nodded. "And I, too, have had enough of him."

"So what now?" said Orthor.

"Good question," said the Red God. She looked around at all the people standing around the table. "All of you except Queen Rhynt and Orthor must go, now and quickly. Follow the rim of the chasm before you to the left. It will take you to the harbor on the other side of the island, and Bebo."

No one moved.

"Why not Queen Rhynt?" said Calax.

"And Orthor?" said Bookins.

"They will serve as bait and distractions from what we must do."

"Bait?" said Bookins. "He hates no one more than me."

"True, but can you read runes?"

"Um, no."

"And that is why Orthor must remain."

"What about me," said the Red Monk. "I have powers, too. I could be of help."

"Alas, no," said the Red God. "The others may need your powers to reach the harbor. Protecting them must be your priority."

"Very well."

"We are wasting time," said Rhynt. "Go, all of you except Orthor."

"But—" said Calax.

"But no," said the queen. "I know I can trust you to see the others to safety. Now go, please."

He nodded. "Very well," he turned to the others. "On me."

Everyone started to move away from the table, but then the roars of the Mercadoos arose from the forest.

"Too late," said Calax, drawing his sword and backing up toward the Summoning Table, along with the others. He turned to the gods. "Do something!"

They looked as frightened as Calax, but the Red God made them move. "Form a circle around them," she said. But the circle never formed. The Black God and the White God disappeared, and the other gods, save for the Red God, were quickly pulled into the forest by the tentacles of what seemed like a hundred Mercadoos.

All was chaos, a state familiar to Calax, Phendour, Blusk, and Priss. They and the queen's hill tigers did their best to protect the others, including the queen and Bookins, pushing them onto the Summoning Table and doing their best to kill any Mercadoo that dared to threaten them.

But there were far too many Mercadoos, far too many. Even Calax, who had dropped into berserker mode, cutting down anything and everything in his path, was having trouble maintaining his balance as the Mercadoos rushed from the forest and up out of the chasm, tentacles shooting out in all directions.

One tentacle shot past Calax's shoulder, and he could hear Ci scream. A second later, the tentacle came back over his shoulder, Ci in its grasp, the Mercadoo dragging her toward the edge of the chasm.

Rhynt couldn't believe her eyes. Little Ci, sweet Ci being dragged over the edge. "No," she screamed, drawing her sword. "Mela, Mila, Spook, to me!"

They raced for the edge, Rhynt swinging her sword at tentacle after tentacle, and leaped into the air. A tentacle shot up at her from the darkness and grasped her leg, and she and her tigers were gone. There was a single scream, and then silence.

As if by signal, the Mercadoos retreated into the jungle and the chasm, leaving Calax and the others gasping for breath.

Calax dropped to his knees and wept.

Phendour and Blusk dropped their swords and put hands on Calax, trying to calm him, but he was inconsolable.

Priss turned away from the others and covered her eyes with her arm to hide her tears, the Red God and the Red Monk beside her, heads down.

Braque and Bookins, who had huddled on the stone together with the others during the battle, shook their heads and patted each other on the back.

Marthe pushed a tear back with a finger and tried to steel himself, but the tears came for him as well, as they did for all his crew.

Orthor walked slowly up to the edge of the chasm and peered down into the darkness. There was nothing.

He turned back to the others. "Just as the runes foretold."

Last Part

What, is that a tear I see? How could you cry at such a wonderful ending? Rhynt and her tigers dead, the others bereft, and me in hot pursuit, ready to end them all. It is the ending I wanted, the ending I expected, the ending the runes foretold.

And yet.

And yet it is not the ending. Ah, you brighten now, as well you should, just as I grow somber and angry.

All right, where was I . . .

121

A roar came up from the chasm, deep and resonant and defiant, but unlike any roar a Mercadoo could manage. A second later, Bebo's head popped up over the edge, and he laughed. "There you are."

As he clambered up over the rim, everyone could see Rhynt and Ci on either shoulder, clinging to his armor, and the three tigers nestled in one arm, as if they were mere kittens.

A cheer went up, and Bebo soon found his legs being hugged by half the people in the clearing.

"Stop, stop," he said. "Must go. All must go."

"What about your joke," said Rhynt.

"No joke now. Elves come. Kill all. Me have joke on ship. Come, run!"

They ran, or at least most of them did. Lord Braque and Bookins fell a few steps behind, but each would later admit that in their relief and giddiness, they had never run so fast in their lives.

Afterword

Of course, they escaped. By the time we reached the clearing, they were long gone. All that remained was a few insolent gods who had been torn to pieces by the Mercadoos. They would piece themselves together, as they always do, but I couldn't have cared less about them.

As for Rhynt and the others, I was not to see them again for many years, but as they say, that is another story.

What I can say is that I learned something valuable, despite the dismal outcome. It is a lesson you should heed as well: never lose track of a troll.

About the Author

Len Boswell is the author of twenty books, including three award-winning series. He lives in the mountains of West Virginia with his wife, Ruth, and their dog Daisy, a beagle who doubles as an avid paper shredder.

Other Titles by Len Boswell

Fantasies:
Barnum's Angel
The Barnacle's Son
The Cave of the Six Arrows
The Fool's Gambit

Simon Grave Mysteries:
A Grave Misunderstanding
Simon Grave and the Curious Incident of the Cat in the Daytime
Simon Grave and the Drone of the Basque Orvilles
Simon Grave and the Sons of Irony
Simon Grave and the School of Casual Invisibility
Simon Grave and the Wrath of Grapes

Other Mysteries:
Flicker: A Paranormal Mystery
Skeleton: A Bare Bones Mystery
Penelope Goodlove's Invisible Detective Agency: The Elephant Who Cried Wolf

Novellas:
LIQ: The Quality of Mercy

Memoirs:
Santa Takes a Tumble
Unboxing Raymond

Nonfiction:
The Leadership Secrets of Squirrels
Stick Figures: The Life and Art of Len Boswell

Note from Len Boswell

Word-of-mouth is crucial for any author to succeed. If you enjoyed *A Rune in Time*, please leave a review online—anywhere you are able. Even if it's just a sentence or two. It would make all the difference and would be very much appreciated.

Thanks!
Len Boswell

We hope you enjoyed reading this title from:

www.blackrosewriting.com

Subscribe to our mailing list – *The Rosevine* – and receive **FREE** books, daily deals, and stay current with news about upcoming
releases and our hottest authors.
Scan the QR code below to sign up.

Already a subscriber? Please accept a sincere thank you for being a fan of
Black Rose Writing authors.

View other Black Rose Writing titles at
www.blackrosewriting.com/books and use promo code
PRINT to receive a **20% discount** when purchasing.